No Man's Land

A Blood Hounds Novel

Ron Schwab

Uplands Press

OMAHA, NEBRASKA

Uplands Press
1401 S 64th Avenue
Omaha, NE 68106
www.uplandspress.com

Publisher's Note: This is a work of fiction. Names, characters, places, and incidents are a product of the author's imagination. Locales and public names are sometimes used for atmospheric purposes. Any resemblance to actual people, living or dead, or to businesses, companies, events, institutions, or locales is completely coincidental.

Ordering Information:
Quantity sales. Special discounts are available on quantity purchases by corporations, associations, and others. For details, contact the "Special Sales Department" at the address above.

Uplands Press / Ron Schwab -- 1st ed.

ISBN 978-1-943421-47-3

Also by Ron Schwab

No Man's Land

A Blood Hounds Novel

Chapter 1

THE MULE TEAM balked at stepping across the railroad tracks, and the bulky, black-bearded buckboard driver cracked his whip to urge them forward. The mules stepped over one rail and onto the railroad bed, then lunged forward to cross the other, with the front wheels creaking and bouncing over the rails until the wagonload of stones spanned the tracks. The driver, Baxter Corker, climbed down from the wagon and with the help of the newest gang member, Moon Parker, an eighteen-year-old Comanche half-blood, began unhitching the mules. That task completed, Parker led the mules away to join the remuda hidden in a draw a quarter mile east of the wagon, nearer to where a section of rail was being removed from the track.

Corker squinted his eyes against the early morning sun's glare, as he watched the wiry "Comanch," as he called the kid, lead the mules past the three men with sledges and bars working a segment of one of the steel rails from the track. He didn't trust the kid. Parker could handle the Colt holstered on his hip better than most, but he was too damn quick to use it. Self-control was not a part of the kid's make-up, and Corker, as a job boss for the overseer, preferred men he could count on to do what they were told. The overseer, Bart Wince, had assigned the kid to Corker's crew, and Corker suspected the half-breed was related to either Wince or "the general," as some referred to the top boss, or to one of their friends. The Comanch just didn't fit the mold of those usually taken into the gang.

The general was a man unknown to all but the overseer, and Corker wasn't certain even Wince knew the leader's identity. Wince had left for Trinidad, Colorado two days earlier to confer with the mystery man who headed up the twenty-some member Blue Bandana Gang. The gang headquartered in Copperhead Canyon at the western end of a public land strip known as "No Man's Land" squeezed between the borders of Texas, Colorado, New Mexico, Kansas and the Indian Territory. The area was not a part of any state or territory, and law was virtually non-existent.

Corker doffed his Plainsman hat and swiped a kerchief over his naked scalp to head off some of the sweat that poured down his face and neck. It was early August on the eastern Colorado plains, and 1882 had turned into a drought year a month back. Today's blazing sun was granting no mercy from the sweltering heat. He pressed the battered hat back on his head and ambled over to check on the rail workers. They had allowed plenty of time. The train owned and operated by the Atchison, Topeka & Santa Fe Railway Company was moving south from Denver and should be swinging east now for its run across Kansas toward Kansas City on the Missouri River. The train should not approach the wagon for an hour or more. Corker had posted a man on a bluff to the west. He would see the engine's billowing stream of smoke miles in the distance as it rolled down the tracks. At first sighting, Jim-Bob Hansen, his lookout, would fire a few shots before mounting his horse and joining the others.

"About got it, Stick?" Corker called to the lean man with a handlebar moustache whose scarecrow frame had earned him his moniker. Some erroneously thought the man's love of dynamite was the name's source. Stick Holdrege was kneeling on the track bed, prying on the last of the rail spikes with an iron bar. Two others waited for the spike's removal before they would use identical bars to lever the rail off the bed.

Stick grunted, and the spike popped up. He stood, picked up a sledge, and hammered the spike free from the rail bracket. "Got the stubborn cuss now," he said, with a deep voice that belied his almost frail appearance. "He weren't givin' up without a fight."

The two other men quickly leveraged their bars under the rail and tipped it away from the bed. No train would be moving beyond this point, if it didn't stop for the wagon.

"I hope they stop the damn train before it gets this far," Corker said, "but we can't chance some engineer thinking he can tear right through the wagon. And I ain't about to show up at Copperhead Canyon without them gold bars."

Stick said, "Boys won't like it if the cars tip over. Make it tougher to take up a collection."

The objective of the robbery was to bring the train to a stop long enough to unload five hundred gold bars secured in a box car on its journey from Denver to the Philadelphia Mint. With the current gold price roughly twenty dollars per ounce, the two-pound bars would be valued easily at an aggregate in excess of $300,000. Another mule team and wagon were hidden in the draw with the horses, and both teams would be hitched to pull the gold bars. They needed to move fast when they pulled away from the train.

Once the wagon was loaded with the gold shipment, the Copperhead crew members were granted twenty minutes to take up their "collection" from the passengers. Money and valuables taken from train occupants would later be split among crew members, a bonus of sorts above and beyond a ten percent cut of the gold heist that would be divided in gold coins after delivery to the general's agents.

"Stick," Corker said, "we're ready. I'm counting on you to blow any locks once we pick out the gold boxcar. You got your dynamite?"

"Ten sticks of the stuff. Part of one will likely do, if I even need it. Got to see the locks before I figure out how to use it. May not even be locked if they got a guard inside."

"I'm waiting here for Jim-Bob to bring word on the train. Take these two and join up with the others at the draw. Tell Gramps I want him on the wagon handling the mules. No collections until the wagon's loaded and ready to go."

"Gotcha, Boss."

Stick and his helpers picked up their tools and headed at a brisk pace toward the robbers' hiding place. Corker paced for a good half hour along the side of the track before he heard two gunshots from the west. He looked toward the hill where Jim-Bob had been posted and saw the young Texan winding down the slope astride his chestnut gelding. Soon, horse and rider hit the flat along the track and were moving at a lope toward Corker.

When Jim-Bob reined in his mount in front of Corker, the rangy tow-headed rider pushed his low-crowned hat back and grinned. "Looks like a long train, Boss." He tapped the telescope poking out of his saddlebags. "I put the spyglass on 'em. Six freight cars, two regular passenger cars and what looked like two Pullman hotel cars and a dining car. There's money riding the rails today. Collections could be good."

"Damn. I don't like so many passengers. Most of the men and a few women will be carrying guns. That ain't good. Ride on down to the draw and tell the boys to be ready for gunplay. And remind them the gold comes first. We might have to forget collections today."

Corker's bay gelding was staked some distance back from the track, and he walked to his mount and hoisted his hefty body into the saddle. Looking over his shoulder for the appearance of the train, he rode along the track to join the other gang members. He had a crew of ten riders besides himself, the gang's other crew having been assigned to strike a string of small town banks along the Colorado-Kansas border.

The general liked to set up same day robberies at different locations with gang members covering their faces with the trademark Indigo blue bandanas that were distributed to each with instructions to wear. Bart said it was a strategy designed to confuse the law, but Corker suspected their leader also loved the notoriety and publicity such stunts earned.

When he reached the draw, Corker confirmed that the men were ready. Gramps McBride, wizened and wrinkled with shaggy, white hair crawling over his shoulders and a tangled beard drooping to his chest, was planted on the buckboard seat, fingers clasped to the mule reins. His double-barreled shotgun was stashed under the seat.

Most of the men had been with the gang several years and went about their jobs in a workmanlike way. He had to keep an eye on Comanch, though, who claimed to be a grandson of the notorious Comanche war chief, Quanah Parker. Corker figured the kid was lying through his teeth and that "Moon Parker" was Comanch's own concoction. He also worried about Comanch's influence on young Jim-Bob, who was a fair gun hand but more like a friendly pup in temperament. Corker wasn't sure Jim-Bob was cut out to be an outlaw, that he had just sort of stumbled into the profession. Jim-Bob had taken to following Comanch like a damned pup, stumbling over his own feet trying to impress the half-blood.

"It's coming, Bax," Stick hollered.

Baxter Corker turned and saw the gray plume of smoke feathering out on the blue horizon above the draw's slope. He swung the bay around and edged the horse out for a look.

Chapter 2

O H, SHIT. THE engineer wasn't slowing. If anything, the train was speeding up. The fool could have made it so easy. The train slows down and stops. The Blue Bandanas ride out and take what they want. Nobody gets hurt.

Corker watched, mesmerized by the approach of the speeding train. Reflexively, he backed away when the engine was only seconds away from the stone-filled buckboard. The crash sounded like the roar of an avalanche exploding off a mountaintop. The engine slammed through the wagon, and huge stones propelled in all directions like cannon balls. But when the engine's wheels struck the gap left by the missing track, it angled left and toppled off the railbed and fell on its side, catapulting one of the occupants through an open window before collapsing on its side.

The coal car and a box car followed before a coupling snapped and the next box car wedged its wheels into the gap and pivoted before tumbling over, landing crossways on the track and blocking the advance of the trailing cars. The next car drove the blockade forward and the remainder of the train folded like an accordion, couplings breaking or disengaging and launching the cars on separate journeys into the adjacent prairielands. When it ended, only a Pullman car and the connected caboose remained on the track, scrunched up against the near-demolished boxcar that had blocked their path. A boxcar and a passenger car remained upright, one on each side of the tracks.

Baxter Corker signaled his gang to move out of the ravine, "Bandanas up men. Keep an eye out for troublemakers. No scavenging or collections until the gold's found and loaded. Keep an eye out for guards."

Corker's crew broke up into pairs to check the boxcars, where the gold bars were likely stashed. The smashed boxcar that had followed the train and coal car was easily removed from the prospect list. It had burst open, and the contents, bundles of beaver, fox, otter and other furs that must have been stacked floor to ceiling, had spilled out on the tracks and surrounding turf.

Corker rode along the near side of the tracks with appraising eyes until he heard gunfire on the far side. He rode up onto a gentle rise and looked in the direction of the racket. The gunshots were coming from the upright passenger car that had ended up some fifty feet from the tracks. The firing was sporadic, so Corker figured there could be no more than two or three guns. Fools. The Bandanas weren't interested in killing anyone who didn't resist. Killings attracted undue attention. Many folks, if their own money was not involved, looked upon bank and train robberies as a sport of sorts, he thought. Many of the gangs, such as the James brothers and the Dalton gang, had robbed their ways to legend in the eyes of some.

Moon Parker and Jim-Bob Hansen had checked the fur-laden boxcar and Corker caught up with them before they joined the others. "Take out the shooters in that passenger car," he said, pointing to where the car rested. For the moment, the gunfire was only a nuisance, since the fire appeared to be coming from handguns without great range or distance accuracy. The two young bandits mounted and reined their horses in the direction of the passenger car.

Now, moans and screaming from the other passenger cars caught Corker's attention. There were obviously injured passengers in the wreckage. Deaths? Nothing to be done about it. He saw several of his crew members scrambling over the remaining wrecked boxcars, tearing locks open with iron bars and sledges retrieved from the buckboard, but the focus appeared to be on the upright boxcar that had rolled to a stop against a cluster of big cottonwoods almost two hundred feet from the tracks. Gramps was heading the wagon in that direction, so Corker reined his gelding across the track and kneed the horse into a lope toward the boxcar.

Stick rode his blue roan gelding out to meet him as he neared. "The treasure's here, Boss. Got to be. Steel-plated door. Locked from the inside, though, so I reckon there's a guard or two in there. Figured to forget about the damn door and just blow out one end."

"You can do it without damage to the bars?"

"Depends on where they're stacked, but at worst, a few would be marked up some. I got a hunch that ain't going to matter to the top dog none."

"Well, get it done. Time's a wasting. And I want to get the hell down the road." He flinched at the incessant shrieking from one of the toppled passenger cars. Then he heard gunfire from the car where he had dispatched the Comanch and Jim-Bob. He saw that his gunmen's horses were hitched at one end of the car, so they had apparently gained access. He was confident any resistors wouldn't be a match for the two young men, but he was mildly surprised when sporadic firing continued. They were likely taking up their collection, and he guessed he wouldn't begrudge them that since they were already in the coach.

He turned back to the boxcar where Stick was anchoring small charges of dynamite along the lower end wall. "Back him up," he hollered at two of his men, who dismounted and trotted to the end of the boxcar with Colts unholstered and ready to fire.

Stick backed away from the car, pulling the fuse with him. He signaled the men to move back, and then he struck a lucifer and lit the fuse. Sputtering fire and smoke began a trek toward the charges. "Take cover, boys," he yelled.

Corker wheeled his mount away none too soon. The blast was ear-shattering, but when he looked back, he saw it had done the job efficiently. All that remained of the end wall was a smoke-filled hole with splintered and ragged edges. "Okay," Corker yelled, "see what we got."

The two men, old hands who went by the names Goose and Rafe, moved forward cautiously, and Stick edged in from the side. Corker slipped his Winchester from its scabbard and levered a cartridge into the chamber. "Anybody in there?" Goose hollered, as he inched near the opening, which was still curtained by smoke. "Speak up. Drop your guns and come out. You won't be harmed."

Silence.

Corker dismounted and moved up next to Stick. "What do you think?"

"Might be nobody. Could be dead. Let the smoke clear some. Just need a few minutes."

Corker was increasingly uneasy about the way the robbery was unfolding. He was distracted for just a bit by terrified screaming and another gunshot from the Comanch's passenger car. He saw Gimpy Smith limping his way, trailed by the Mexican, Pete Morales, leading two horses. That left Bull Killer and Smoke Brown unaccounted for, likely starting their looting of the passenger cars early. Sometimes he felt like he was working with a bunch of damned thieves who had no scruples at all.

"Okay," Stick said. "Move in careful-like, boys."

Rafe, younger and more agile than the tall, beefy Goose, climbed upon the coupling and peered in the car just before the roar of a shotgun echoed and sent a full load of shot into his gut, dropping him like a sack of potatoes off his perch. A second blast tore into Goose's shoulder and spun him around before he took a few steps and fell, facedown, in the dust.

Stick stepped out, fired a few quick shots with his Colt and ducked back just in time to evade another shotgun burst. "I think there's at least two in there, Bax," he told Corker.

"Shit. Any ideas?"

"Yep. I just toss 'em a little stick of my candy and blow 'em to hell. Bars might get scattered or damaged some, but I don't think you're wanting to try to out wait the crazy bastards."

"You got that right. I'll give them one last chance." Taking care not to expose himself to an itchy trigger finger, he yelled from the side of the car. "Hey, you, in there. Come out with hands raised high, and you'll live. Otherwise, you're good as dead."

Silence.

"Okay, Stick, give the varmints your medicine."

"They're getting a full dose. You'll want to get Rafe and Goose out of here."

Corker yelled at the newcomers, who had been chatting with Gramps, who was some distance away with the buckboard and mule teams. "Gimp, Morales. Get off your fat asses and move Rafe and Goose over by the wagon."

Gimpy Smith, a thickly muscled man in his early forties, and Pete Morales, a shorter, stocky man about the same age, dragged the wounded men away, although

Gimpy took a scattering of buckshot in his ribs when one of the shotguns blasted again. Corker noticed that Goose seemed to be coming around, but Rafe seemed to be breathing, and that was about all.

"Ready?" Stick asked.

Corker sighed, "Yeah. Let's do it."

"Get going."

Corker snatched his gelding's reins and started stumbling toward the buckboard, huffing and wheezing as he moved at a pace that would barely pass for running. He was a man who was accustomed to moving on his butt, astride a good horse. He paused to catch his breath and cast a look over his shoulder. He saw Stick light his candle, toss it in the boxcar and start to run. What in the hell? The dynamite stick came flying back out. Corker turned and started rushing for the wagon again.

The explosion showered him with dirt and stones, but he kept his footing, as he came up to the wagon and grabbed a sideboard for support. The mules were restless, but Gramps had them under control. Where was Stick? He looked back toward the boxcar, searching through the haze of smoke and dust for a spell before he saw Stick's slender form stretched out on the ground. "Gimp," he said, "you come along and cover me in case one of them bastards takes a notion to try some sniping.

Pete, you round up the others. All of them. Collections are done for the day. We gotta grab this gold and git."

Morales hurried off to find the other gang members, while Corker, trailed by Gimpy, circled away from the boxcar's shattered backside and crept toward Stick, who was struggling to right himself now. Keeping an eye on the boxcar, he slipped in beside his old friend and knelt.

"You going to be all right?" Corker asked.

Stick lifted himself to his hands and knees. "Got the dang wind knocked plumb out of me. I oughta be dead." Gimpy and Corker helped the man stagger to his feet and assisted him to the buckboard, where they eased him to the ground, leaning against a spoked wagon wheel.

Corker said, "Blew quite a hole in the ground with that stick they fired back."

Stick said, "Somebody must have caught the damned thing and throwed it right back. That was a short-fused stick."

"I never seen such a thing. If they'd have give up the fight, the worst they'd got was a tap on the head. We got no choice now but to take 'em out."

"Bax?"

It was Gramps. "Yeah. What is it?"

"You'd better take a look at Rafe."

The wounded men had been laid out on the ground on the opposite side of the wagon, so Corker walked around to check on their condition. Goose Hanshaw was sitting up now, his shoulder wrapped with blood-soaked rags salvaged from the man's shirt. Gramps said, "Nothing busted up. Buckshot tore up the shoulder but shouldn't kill old Goose. He's got plenty of meat about the neck and shoulder. Need to pluck out some shot later and clean up the mess, but if it don't putrefy, he'll make it."

Corker stepped over to Rafe and knelt beside him. He saw instantly that the wounded man would not be riding away with his comrades. The man moaned and sobbed in agony and his eyes were glazed over like those of a man on the trail to the end. Corker inched his fingers under the rags that wrapped Rafe's midsection and tugged them up, so he could examine the wounds. The flesh of the abdomen was shredded, and Rafe's bloody, torn intestines bulged through the cavity. It was only a matter of time. But how long would the dying take? The Blue Bandana Gang's policy was simple: no live gang member was to be left behind. Accordingly, Rafe's inability to travel imposed a duty upon the crew leader.

"Move Goose away from here," Corker ordered.

Gimpy and Gramps helped Goose Hanshaw to his feet and walked him to the wagon, boosting him to the rear of the box to sit. Corker slipped his Navy Colt from its holster and pressed the barrel tip against the thrashing Rafe's temple before he squeezed the trigger. The resulting explosion spattered the crew leader's face with blood, bone splinters and brain mush, and, as he stood, he wiped his face and beard with his shirtsleeve and shrugged. He told himself it was an act of mercy. He would have done the same for a horse.

Regardless, the gang could not run the risk of Rafe lingering long enough to divulge the location of Copperhead Canyon or other details regarding the gang's operations. He had done what he had been instructed to do on at least two other occasions. He assumed this would not be the last.

Corker looked back toward the wreckage and saw Morales trotting toward him, followed by Smoke Brown and Bull Killer, walking behind at a slower pace. Smoke, an African apparently untainted by white blood in his lineage, had been born and spent his early childhood as a slave in Alabama, and that was all Corker knew about his past. Bull Killer, a few inches shorter than the six and a half feet tall Smoke, was also an enigma when it came to his past. He claimed to be an eastern Indian. Corker thought one of the men had said, "Huron," or something of the sort. The pair had shown up at the canyon together several years earlier, both early thirties, lean, sinewy and strong enough to be yoked like oxen to pull a loaded Conestoga. The two shared one of the crude log cabins near the far end of the blind canyon and kept to themselves, except when the crew was on a mission. A willowy, exotic-looking mulatto woman, Minnie, had come with them and looked after the one-room cabin and did their cooking, laundry and whatever else they had brought her along for. Strange situation, Corker thought. Made him curious and a little horny thinking about what might go on there. None of his concern. The odd pair were reliable with their weapons and fierce in a fight. Did what was asked of them. That's all Corker cared about.

"Where's the Comanch and Jim-Bob?" Corker asked, as Morales approached.

Morales rolled his eyes, and he seemed to be searching for words. "Moon, he say they come soon."

Corker fumed. "What are they doing?"

"They have a girl."

"A girl? What do you mean?"

"They . . . they use her. You know what I mean?"

Just what they needed. From the gunfire, he suspected passengers had been killed. A rape would be even worse and turn public opinion totally against them. Train robbery would cease to be looked upon as sport. They had to get this job done and get the hell out. Corker figured he'd let Bart Wince, the overseer, deal with Moon and Jim-Bob.

When Smoke and Bull Killer arrived, Corker pointed at the boxcar's open end and said, "There's two guards in there. We got to take 'em out. Now. A rain of fire. Get some cover out of shotgun range and start pouring on the lead."

The men retrieved their rifles from their saddle holsters and took up positions on a hillock out of lethal shotgun range. Morales and the other two flattened their bodies against the rocky ground and readied their rifles to fire.

"Go ahead," Corker said, "time's wasting."

The first rifle cracks were almost simultaneous. After that, the fire became more sporadic but unceasing until Corker figured sixty or seventy rounds had been fired and directed a halt.

"What do you think, Pete?" he asked.

"Cannot say. Too dark at front end of the car. Hiding behind gold stack, I think."

"Ricochets should have taken them out."

Suddenly, one of the guards appeared at the opening of the boxcar, gray shirt splotched with blood, staggering with a shaky hand clutching a pistol and eyes searching out a target. Smoke and Bull Killer commenced firing again, their sure aims launching lead that riddled the guard's torso. The body crumpled and tumbled off the rear of the car.

"Okay," Corker said, "move in slow-like, and make certain the other's not playing possum someplace. Then we got us work to do."

Morales, Smoke and Bull Killer spread out and walked down the slope toward the boxcar, rifles ready to fire. There was no response to their movement, and when they reached the boxcar, Bull Killer leaped inside and disappeared, while his comrades backed him from outside. A prolonged silence encouraged Corker. At least the resistance appeared finished. When the Indian returned, he nodded at Corker. "Guard's dead."

Morales was leaning over the body sprawled on the ground outside the boxcar and called to Corker, "Bax, you'd better take a look at this."

Corker didn't like the sound of the Mexican's voice and headed toward the boxcar. "What is it?" Corker grumbled when he stepped up next to Morales.

"Look."

The guard's body lay face up, and he saw a silver badge glinting in the sun's rays. And he realized they had killed a woman, a very pretty one with black hair and olive-tinted skin. He knelt beside her and removed the badge, studying it and reading the words aloud. "Pinkerton National Detective Agency."

He tossed the badge in the dirt beside the dead woman, trying to convince himself things couldn't get worse. He knew the Pinkertons only by reputation, but from all he had heard, he thought he'd rather have the Army or U. S. Marshals Service on their tails. Killing of a woman, and a Pinkerton no less, was going to bring trouble. Big trouble.

Then things got worse.

Chapter 3

OON PARKER AND Jim-Bob Hansen reined their mounts in near the boxcar. Blue bandanas still covered their faces, but the rest of the crew had by now tugged the uncomfortable masks off. That would not ordinarily have been a problem, but the Comanch had a young woman, more girl, Corker guessed, slung sideways across his lap. Parker slid his captive off the horse and let her drop on the ground. Surprisingly, she did not cry out.

She scrambled to her feet, planted her hands on her hips and glared at Corker defiantly. She was afraid, but, somehow, she had subdued the fear in those green eyes. Kind of a skinny kid, he thought. Tall, chestnut-colored hair that fell to her shoulders but looked like a tangled bird's nest right now. Her cheek was swollen, her lip bleeding. Dress half torn away. She would clean up more than nice, but the Comanch, and maybe Jim-Bob, too, had roughed her up, likely had their ways with her, probably more than once.

He turned back to Morales, who was watching silently. "Pete, the rest of you get the wagon up here and load the gold. I got to have me a talk with these damned idiots."

After Morales and the others left, Corker confronted the two latecomers. "Get out of your saddles, both of you. I ain't messing around with you no more. Stay put and pray I don't kill you." He looked at the girl, who was obviously sizing up the situation. The fools hadn't taken off with some feeble-minded nitwit. That made her more dangerous.

Corker asked, "How old are you, girl?"

"Fifteen last week." Her voice was soft but steady.

"What's your name?"

"Maddie Sanford."

Shit. Don't let it be. "You related to the railroad Sanfords?"

"My father's a vice-president of the AT & SF. One of the shareholders."

"Did these men violate you?"

She looked uncertainly at Moon Parker. "He did. Twice. The other one didn't touch me. He tried to stop it but gave up easy."

"I wasn't her first time," Parker said. "I could tell."

"Jim-Bob, get your ass out of here and help load that wagon," Corker ordered.

Corker thought Jim-Bob was scared shitless and glad to be on his way. He wasn't done with him, but he wanted to go one on one with the Comanch. He slid his Colt from its holster and pointed the weapon at Moon Parker. "Now, Comanch, I want you to unbuckle your gun belt and drop it on the ground. Don't get any fool ideas, or you're coyote food. You're likely faster on the draw than me, but not when I got the drop on you."

"I don't get this. Why? I didn't do nothin'. I just got me a woman. Smoke and Bull Killer got their own woman. I get tired of those three worn out whores you got up at the canyon."

"The gun belt. Now."

He unbuckled the belt and let it drop with the two holstered Colts at his feet.

Corker turned to Maddie Sanford. "Ma'am, can you ride a horse decent?"

"Yes. More than decent."

"You don't need one of them side saddles?"

"Never used one."

"You take the reins of this grasshopper brain's paint. That little gelding's as good as we got."

"But I want to stay with the train."

"Can't do it, ma'am. Unless I leave you dead. You seen the faces of most of our men. Seeing one's usually a death sentence. But you come along without a fuss, and you might find your way home yet. I promise this man won't bother you again. If he tries, his dried-out balls will hang on my lodge door. You do what you're told, and no man touches you. Understand?"

"I understand." She stepped over and clutched the reins of Parker's mount and led the horse away from its owner.

"Now, Comanch," Corker said, "you can take Rafe's gelding or walk, but get your ass over there and help load that wagon."

"I got a collection in my saddle bags," Parker whined.

"It ain't going nowhere. We'll look at it and make a split when we get to Copperhead Canyon. You've caused some serious trouble. Bart's gonna be the one to decide what to do about it, if I don't kill you first."

The young man's dark eyes widened. "What do you mean, kill me?"

"Just what I said. If I was you, I'd start being a good boy and doing what you're told."

"My guns."

"I'll take good care of them. Now, git."

Corker's eyes followed the Comanch, as he walked away with his head down like a whipped pup, finally disappearing behind the boxcar. He turned back to the girl, who stood no more than ten paces away, her hand grasping the paint's reins. She was staring at him but not with fear in her eyes. He sensed that she was appraising him, taking inventory of what she was up against. Damn it. He would have to keep a close eye on this filly, probably tie her up at night. He walked to the paint gelding and pulled the Comanch's Winchester from its scabbard. He supposed a rich girl like this wouldn't know how to use the thing, but he wasn't taking any chances.

An hour later, the Blue Bandana Gang rode away from the train wreck, heading south toward the Cimarron River. There, they would divide up the gold bars and place them onto canvas-wrapped racks and load the bounty onto the four mules, two-hundred-fifty pounds each. This would be a manageable burden for the pack animals and would not slow the outlaws' pace significantly. The buckboard would be abandoned in the river and hopefully the current would carry it east downstream a good distance. The Blue Bandana riders would travel west for a good spell in the shallows of the river channel, to wash away their trail. A two-day trip would take them to the west end of No Man's Land, less than ten miles from New

Mexico Territory border where their hideout, dubbed "Copperhead Canyon" for its infestation of serpentine occupants, was located.

Baxter Corker was confident they would easily be ensconced in the nearly impregnable natural fortress of the canyon before the law could be organized for pursuit. And who had jurisdiction in No Man's Land? The uncertain answer to that question provided a convenient excuse for a tired posse to pull back and abandon the chase. His larger concern was long term. What action might the killings trigger?

And then there was the girl. They could not cut her loose. He supposed Maddie Sanford would be a prime hostage if the robbery precipitated a crisis. She, of course, was merchandise for a ransom, but could they risk an exchange that would set her mouth free? He sighed. He hated like hell to report to Bart Wince, who would be pissed that the overseer would be forced to carry bad news to the general, who was unknown to anyone else and was located someplace west.

Chapter 4

AUGUST 28, 1882. Today Darby Kathleen Maguire Crockett would celebrate two months of marriage to John Trace Crockett. Of course, Trace would not have a clue. She stretched like a sleepy cat on the straw mattress that covered the warped cedar floor before rolling over on her belly, resting her head on folded arms and watching the naked man who lay no more than two feet away. He was a ruggedly handsome prize, she thought, the morning stubble shadowing Trace's dark cheeks and his eyes closed in slumber. Her eyes shifted to the broad, shoulders and roamed over the muscled torso, lightly cloaked with wayward curls of hair and rising and falling gently as he slumbered. The bedsheet barely reached his waist and was tented by what lay beneath. She wondered if he was dreaming of his wife. Or was it some slut from his past teasing him now?

The fingers of sunlight were creeping through the dust-coated window now, and the room was already hot and muggy. Trace had assured her that dugouts were cool in summer and warm in winter when they purchased the two sections of land in the Kansas Flint Hills with their partner, Audra Scott, little more than a month ago. Trace had convinced her that temporarily putting up with the primitive living quarters left money to buy more acres. Darby admitted, tight fisted as she was with money, she had willingly bought in to the idea. Damn, he was on to her, appealing to her frugality when it worked his way. She had known when she impulsively agreed to marry him after less than three weeks acquaintance that she was buying into a financial tug of war with the free-spending Trace. Love had caught her totally off guard when she had teamed with fellow Pinkerton operative, Trace Crockett, on one of the detective agency's missions. She must have been insane. Perhaps her brain had been numbed from the severe beating she had taken during the mission.

She sighed and pushed herself upon her knees. And now she knew she could not live without him. But she should celebrate their anniversary. She reached over and pulled down the sheet that covered Trace and eased on top of him. His eyes opened, and he tendered that knowing, crooked grin. "Don't you dare say a word," Darby warned, before she kissed him and set about her business.

Afterward, they lay side by side on the mattress, sweat-soaked and fingers entwined, staring at the oak-beamed ceiling that was sheathed with pine planks that admitted slivers of light. Trace had purchased several buckets of pine tar a week ago, promising he would get the cracks sealed before another deluge like the one a few weeks earlier that had left everything in the two-room cabin drenched. They had escaped a total soaking by stringing a canvas tarp from the ceiling and anchoring the sides to the walls to form a tent over the mattress.

"I'll help you seal the roof today," Darby said.

"Well," Trace said, "I don't know. It doesn't look like rain and I'd like to fix some fence."

"Trace, we don't even own one cow. To hell with the fence. Let's get the roof done today. I don't want to move to town."

"You're saying you'd leave me over the roof."

"I just won't stay here with the roof like this. I'll come visit, sometimes."

He chuckled and rolled over on his side, facing her and running his fingers through her long wheat-gold hair. "Bet you'd visit a lot."

"Maybe not as much as you think."

Trace leaned over and kissed her behind the ear. "I'm going to get up and get a fire going in the fireplace, and we can make some coffee and warm up the biscuits left over from last night. Then I'll get started on the roof."

"Do you mean that?"

"I do. Anything to keep my woman happy."

He climbed out of bed, and, without even pulling on his undershorts, opened the door and stepped into the living area. Darby figured he was showing off. Trace was six feet, two inches tall and didn't carry an ounce of fat, and she didn't mind the sight of her husband's nice butt as he slipped out the door.

Then she heard a familiar voice. "Trace, we really shouldn't be meeting like this."

"Oh, damn. How long have you been out here?"

"Long enough. I hammered on the door. You didn't answer, so I let myself in. I own this place, too, you know."

"The door was locked."

"Have you ever seen a lock stop me? Then, I got in and realized you were busy, so I just sat down to wait. You weren't that noisy, if that's what you're worried about."

"I'm not worried, but you could have called out."

"Go make yourself decent and get Darby out here. I've got some news."

Audra. It was a half hour ride from Manhattan. What was she doing at the so-called ranch this early in the morning?

Chapter 5

WHEN TRACE REENTERED the bedroom to get dressed, Darby was already buttoning her shirt. "It's Audra," he said. "She said she has some news."

"I heard. Get yourself covered for God's sake. We can't be running around the house like a pair of naked jaybirds anymore," she said in a near whisper.

"I don't think Audra gave it much of a thought."

"Maybe not. But it could have been anybody."

"Not sitting in the front room."

"Well, it's not very professional."

Trace shrugged. If Darby disapproved of any specific conduct, she tended to label it "unprofessional." Sometimes he struggled to know what in the hell she was talking about, but he just took it as an endearing quirk.

Darby pulled on her faded Levi's jeans and headed barefoot for the living area. Trace tugged on his britches and yesterday's shirt. Teased by Darby and Audra for his fastidious ways, he expected to shave later and bathe at the little waterfall that tumbled over a limestone wall some fifty yards from the cabin and pooled before overflowing and snaking its way to a creek in the valley. The stream was spring fed and ice-cold but a lot more convenient than pumping and boiling water for the washtub, which was usually Darby's preference even though she could barely squeeze into the rusting tin tub. She stood five and a half feet tall but was slender as a reed. With winter only a few months away, they had to figure out a bathing alternative soon. He would never fit in the tub. Occasionally, on a hot day, Darby might join him in the pool. Maybe he could entice her to the falls today.

He was not embarrassed about encountering Audra outside their room. She was a former prostitute and had been an occasional thief on the side before signing on with the Crockett Detective Agency, and unbeknownst to Darby, the two had shared a night of intimacy before Trace met his future wife. Also, the three had camped together on the trail, where modesty tended to give way to practicality.

When he walked out of the bedroom, Darby already had a little flame nipping at the twigs in the fireplace, and Audra was placing seven leftover biscuits in the Dutch oven to warm up. He didn't mind the extra warmth tossed off by the fireplace. Trace thrived in heat, but he suspected his companions would be suffering a bit. He opened the room's two windows wider, but it likely would not help much.

Soon the three were gathered around the little kitchen table with a pot of hot coffee, a plate of biscuits, bowl of butter and jar of honey. Trace stared at the sable-haired Audra, stunning as usual with her lively dark eyes and flawless, lightly bronzed skin. "Well," he said, "you have news. You rode all the way out here to deliver it. Would you like to tell us?"

She finished a biscuit and began buttering another. The tiny young woman, who might reach five feet and tip the scales at a bit over a hundred pounds, ate like a horse and loved to torment him.

"I got a telegram before I left the office last night, but I didn't think it made sense to ride out after dark. With all due respect, I have nicer accommodations, and I didn't know where you'd put me if I stayed over."

She was referring to her lodging at the luxurious Wheaton mansion, where she had been invited to stay on indefinitely after helping with recovery of the missing heiress, Miranda Wheaton. "Just tell us," Trace growled.

"We have a visitor from the Pinkerton Kansas City office coming in on the train this afternoon. He should be in Manhattan by two o'clock."

"Carl Chirnside?"

"Yeah. How did you know?"

"He's the only occupant of the office. Manager, agent, clerk, janitor. A man of many titles."

Audra wolfed down her second biscuit. "There's one left. Anybody going to eat it?" She didn't wait for an answer and plucked the biscuit from the plate.

Darby asked Trace, "Chirnside wouldn't be making a personal visit for a routine job, would he?"

"Not likely. This might be where our contract decision will pay off, if you can negotiate the right deal."

Trace hated dickering with folks about money, and Darby thrived on the game, so he willingly ceded such responsibilities to his new wife. They needed every nickel they could squeeze out of a Pinkerton assignment. Both Trace and Darby had been salaried operatives, but that meant taking whatever job the Chicago home office assigned. The result could have resulted in prolonged separation. Instead, after forming a friendship with Audra Scott during their previous assignment, they had invited her to join them in a new detective agency located in Manhattan, Kansas, where the three had already pooled funds to invest in ranch land in the surrounding Flint Hills.

Trace, closing in on his twenty-ninth birthday, had been raised on a Tennessee ranch, lost by his father in the aftermath of the Civil War, and dreamed of establishing a thriving ranch in tallgrass country. The ranch, dubbed "Three Winds Ranch" by the owners, had been purchased without borrowing funds, but the investors had been left land poor, a not uncommon plight for folks who farmed or ranched. With the land as security, they could likely mortgage the land to acquire two hundred cows to stock the place, but it would take several years to generate significant cash flow. This made the agency's success imperative for the indefinite future.

Allan Pinkerton and his sons, Robert and William, had initially been cool to the new agency's proposal to work for the firm on a contract basis. This meant the fledgling Crockett Detective Agency would retain the right to reject assignments and that fees would be negotiated and agreed upon on a case by case basis. Finally, the Pinkertons had agreed to an affiliation that would continue only so long as the Crockett agency worked exclusively for Pinkerton National. Crockett operatives would be required to carry Pinkerton credentials and badges on their assignments.

In effect, the Manhattan detectives were still Pinkertons with an illusory independence. The downside was that Pinkerton had yet to offer an assignment, and, unlike their previous status as employees, Trace and Darby had no salary to keep them afloat during slack times. They suspected Allan Pinkerton had been sending a silent message about his former employees' move toward independence. Trace had been ready to tell Allan to go to hell and commence soliciting customers in competition with Pinkerton, but Darby had counseled patience, assuring him she had squirreled away funds that would keep them eating through the winter. It seemed she was always coming up with money he didn't know about.

Trace finished his coffee and scooted his chair back from the table. "If Chirnside's coming, I won't have time to do the work on the roof today. Sorry, Darb."

"I can see you're disappointed."

Trace did not miss her sarcasm. "I know you want that fixed, Love. And I'd really planned to get on it."

Audra chimed in. "You mean after that mess you had in here after the storm, you haven't fixed the roof?"

"Thanks, Audra," Trace said.

"I was going to help him today," Darby said.

"Jimmy Dale would do it, and it wouldn't cost you an arm and a leg. He does odd jobs all over Manhattan. Suzanne has him painting the interior of her barber shop today. You can catch him when you come to town. I'll bet he'd be out here in a day or two. He's a first-rate handyman. He'll do a good job."

"That's what I need," Darby said. "A man who's handy."

Trace decided not to remind her that she had not complained about his handiness when she woke up this morning. Trace stood. "Well, I've got to shave and head over to the falls for a bath. Hope I've got something decent to wear out here. All my best suits are still stored in town. I really need a new suit." Darby's coffee-brown eyes shot daggers, and he decided not to press the issue.

Audra said, "I'll be at the office at one o'clock in case Mister Chirnside shows up early." She got up. "I've got to ride. I'm meeting Suzy for breakfast at The Chuck Wagon. Flapjacks special all morning."

Trace said, "You already had breakfast."

Audra ignored him.

Suzy was Suzanne Carter, like Audra, a onetime prostitute, who was two or three years younger than Audra's twenty-three. They had both plied their trade at a bordello in Stone Creek, a small cow town located in an area called No Man's Land. Audra had catered to wealthy clients, and the enterprising Suzanne had fashioned a career as a barber at the bordello, known as "The Manor," before they both moved on and escaped the tragic fate of so many whose circumstances pressed them to the profession. Suzanne was now their landlord, sharing the building where her barbershop was located with Crockett Detective Services.

After Audra went out the door, Trace stood in the doorway, watching his young friend step into the saddle of her Appaloosa mare and rein the horse northwest toward town. He felt Darby's hand slip around his waist, and he looked down at her and met her gaze. She was amused about something. "What?" he asked.

"You've slept with Audra, haven't you? I can tell. Neither one of you hides it well."

He rolled his eyes. He and Audra had made a pact. They would never tell Darby. "I love you, Darb. How about taking a bath with me at the falls this morning?"

She smiled. "I need one after a night with you. I smell like a cow."

"I don't know how to take that, but I'll be glad for your company. While we're there, maybe we can talk about a new bathtub."

Chapter 6

DARBY DISMOUNTED IN front of the small limestone building, and Trace took the reins of her blood bay mare, Cinnamon, and rode on toward the livery, where he would leave the mare and his big buckskin stallion, Atlas, for the afternoon. Trace was glad to handle stable duty because Darby was planning to stop at Suzy's Shearing and hire Jimmy Dale to repair the roof. He applauded the plan, but he did not want to listen to her badger the young man into underpricing his work.

When he returned to the building, he entered the Crockett offices and found Audra, attired in a blue business jacket and matching skirt, sitting at her desk and typing something on the Remington. She seemed to look for excuses to type on the machine, which he wanted nothing to do with, and her fingers moved over the keys with the speed of a bullet.

"Darb's obviously still next door talking to Jimmy Dale," he remarked.

She stopped typing. "Oh," she said. "I didn't know she was over there. I hope she can work something out with him. You shouldn't let that roof go."

"I know. I'd like to put up a new house on the place. Just something small that we can add on to when we've got the money. Convincing Darb to spend the money's going to take some doing, though."

"She'll come around. You do make a good team, you know. You might tug different ways, but you end up in the middle and don't let differences turn nasty. Early on, I saw it. You two like each other. You're friends. When the chips are down, you've got each other's backs. Love is the sweet bonus. And, if you decide to build, I'll deed off my interest in a parcel for a house."

"Yeah, I guess you're right." Of course, he could say much the same about Audra, leaving off the bonus. The three were friends, the kind each could count on.

The door opened, and Darby walked in with a satisfied smile on her face. "Jimmy's going to take care of the roof day after tomorrow. He'll see if he can do anything else to get the place fit for winter, too. I took so long because I asked him if he thought he could build a house next spring. It turns out that's his dream. To start his own company and build houses. He'd give us a special break on price if he could build one for us to prove to folks he can do it."

Trace was stunned. "You're willing to build a house out there?"

"Well, not a big house. Two bedrooms, so Audra can stay over when she wants. Separate kitchen and parlor. And I want a water closet for a big bathtub. Jimmy's been studying about plumbing, and he knows he can get a line from the well, so we can pump water in the kitchen sink, and he can put a tank for storing water outside the house for the bathtub. And he thinks we might even be able to have a flush stool in the water closet if he can figure out how to get through the rock out there to drain the stool and tub. I told him to look over the area near the cabin and suggest where he might put a house. I want to know what he can do with a budget of five thousand dollars before we decide." She looked at Trace. "I know I should have discussed this with you, Trace. We might need to borrow for some of the cost. It won't go any farther without your say-so. I just thought I'd inquire."

"No. No. That's fine. This is something we should probably be thinking about." He glanced at Audra, who gave him a quick wink. "Plumbing to the house. Now that would be a luxury for anybody outside of town, and most in."

"We'll see. It can't hurt to look at his ideas," Darby said. "Now, I need to get out of my riding clothes and into something more professional. I've got some clothes in the backroom closet, so I'm going to make a change. I suppose we'll meet in the conference room."

"It's ready," Audra said.

There was not much to get ready. The building had three rooms: the storage room where Darby was headed, the front room, where each of the three partners had a separate desk to work at, and the conference room, barely large enough to hold a small library table and six chairs. Several empty filing cabinets sat against the wall in the front room, and they didn't require much else, certainly not until they had some bona fide clients. Hopefully today would bring the client they had been waiting for.

When Darby appeared fifteen minutes later, she had transformed from a cowgirl in boots and jeans, to a businesswoman in high button shoes and conservative gray skirt and jacket. She also wore her wire-rimmed spectacles.

Trace had donned his rust-brown pinstripe suit at the cabin and wore freshly polished brown boots. Darby always teased him that he had three times the number of boots than she had shoes, but he admitted to a penchant for fine boots and a fashionable wardrobe in general, for that matter. He would need to broach her about the topic of ample closet space in the new home she was proposing.

Shortly before two o'clock, the office door creaked open, and a short, ruddy-faced man with a belly that lopped over his belt limped in, lugging a battered and bulging leather briefcase. He removed his hat, revealing a few patches of white hair on an otherwise smooth scalp. His rumpled suit showed the effects of some hours of train travel. Trace stepped forward to greet his old friend and Pinkerton supervisor.

"Carl. Welcome to Manhattan." They exchanged firm handshakes, and Trace introduced Carl Chirnside to Darby and Audra before escorting the visitor to the conference room.

Chirnside dropped his briefcase on the table and opened it before sitting down. "If you take the job, I'll be leaving bag and contents with you."

Trace knew Darby would be champing at the bit to dive into the mass of paper. She thrived on examining and analyzing documents. He did not. "Tell us about the job."

"In a moment. First, a few questions. Would you be willing to hire another man for the assignment? Pinkerton would include salary costs in the contract, of course."

Trace looked at his partners for their reactions and received two shrugs. "I don't see why not, but it might take time to find somebody."

"I've got the somebody. Do you have a problem working with a Negro?"

"Of course not. I served as a sergeant with Mackenzie during the Red River war. He had the Ninth and Tenth Cavalry buffalo soldiers under his command. No better men."

"Well, I guess he's a Negro. That's what it shows on the Pinkerton records. He must be half-blood Cherokee because he told me his mother's full blood. I guess a lot of slaves found their way to the Cherokees before the war. Some were freemen, others became Cherokee slaves. I don't understand how it all came to be. Anyway, he will be African for this assignment."

Audra chimed in, "I'm quarter blood Cherokee. My mother was half blood. This office doesn't keep track of bloodlines, I promise you."

"His name is Clayton Sibley. He goes by Clay. He'd be early thirties, a few years older than you, Trace. He was a buffalo soldier with the Tenth. Fought Comanches in

Texas, but I don't think your service time overlapped. He joined the Pinkertons before you went on active duty. You've never met him because he's been an operative out of the Chicago office, mostly on northeastern assignments. He's been itching for advancement, and I thought he was a perfect fit for what we've got in mind. Allan's not sure he can keep the guy happy, so he wouldn't be upset if your agency took him over when this project's done."

"So, when do we meet this gentleman?"

Chirnside slid his chair back from the table and sighed deeply as he stood up and walked stiff-legged out of the conference room door. While the Pinkerton manager was absent, Trace informed his partners, "Carl's been with the Pinkerton Agency from the beginning, over thirty years now. He hasn't taken many operative assignments because of the bad knee. He took a gunshot there when the Pinkertons were handling Lincoln's protection early in the war. The would-be assassins didn't reach the President that time, as Allan Pinkerton takes every opportunity to remind everyone."

A few minutes later, Chirnside reappeared, followed by a well-dressed man in a business suit that could not hide the muscular physique it covered. Trace put him at about six-feet tall, a few inches shorter than himself. Copper skin and an aquiline nose, perhaps reflecting his

Cherokee heritage. Clean shaven. Short-cropped hair hinting African texture. Melting pot American with a spice of ancestry that was tougher to escape than most. Most women, unless blinded by prejudice, would gape in awe at Clay Sibley, Trace figured.

Trace got up and stepped around the table and extended his hand, receiving a grip that was just short of bone-crunching. "Clay, it's our pleasure to welcome you to our outfit. I'm Trace Crockett and to my right is my wife and business partner, Darby, and opposite her is our partner, Audra Scott."

Clay said, "Pleased to meet you, Trace." He nodded and tendered Darby and Audra a shy smile. "And you, ladies."

Chirnside sat down and signaled Clay to do the same. The newcomer took the vacant chair adjacent to Audra, whose petite form seemed even tinier next to the muscular Clay Sibley.

Chirnside took charge. "I'll tell you about the assignment. If we come to terms, I'll leave all the information in the briefcase behind, and you can read everything the Chicago office has collected." His fierce blue eyes locked on Trace's. "You've heard of the Blue Bandana gang?"

"Yeah. They make the headlines almost weekly these days. A week or so ago, they took out an AT & SF train in eastern Colorado, made off with a gold shipment and killed a half dozen people. Twice that were injured by either gunshot or train derailment. Details have been sort of foggy."

"Railroad's telling as little as possible for reasons I'll explain shortly. Yes. This gang seems to be everyplace. Sometimes, a bank or train gets robbed a hundred miles apart on the same day. Either there is an imposter gang or they're a big outfit able to send out two different groups. They hadn't done a lot of killing until the AT & SF robbery last week. And this was their biggest haul—over three hundred thousand dollars in gold bullion."

"My God." Trace said. "Who would be hauling that much gold in a single load on a train?"

"The United States government, that's who. A shipment from Denver to the Philadelphia Mint."

"It's insane to put that many eggs in a basket."

"You're talking about government bureaucrats. Insanity is routine. But that's not the worst of it."

"Go on."

"The Pinkerton Agency was hired to guard the bullion. Two agents were killed. Martin Jacobs and Mary Lange."

"No," Darby groaned, "I knew Mary when I was with the Denver office. Such a good, kind person."

"They apparently put up a bitter fight. The boxcar was riddled with lead. Mary's body was found outside. Shot twenty times or more. Looked like she went down firing. They must have refused to surrender. Needless to say, Allan wants to take down the killers."

"What about the liability for the gold?" Trace asked.

"The agency gets a release before taking on these assignments. No guarantees of safe delivery. But the loss can cost Pinkerton future jobs." He hesitated. "There's more. The train robbers abducted a fifteen-year-old girl. Name's Maddie Sanford. Happens to be an AT & SF vice-president's daughter. A passenger says the girl was also raped."

"Damn," Trace said. "The bastards. None of this has been reported that I've seen. Neither the gold nor the girl."

"It'll leak out, but the railroad and the government are keeping a cover on it for now. There's the embarrassment and, understandably, puzzlement about the girl's safety. No ransom demand's been made the last I knew—and she's as good as more bullion. The father could probably scratch up fifty thousand if he sold his company shares. The Santa Fe would probably back him for that much, too." The Atchison, Topeka and Santa Fe Railway Company was commonly referred to as AT & SF or, alternatively, Santa Fe.

Darby asked, "Do you think she was part of the plan?"

"I doubt it. Our information was that her mother put her on the train in Denver. She'd been a problem and was being sent to her father in Kansas City. The father didn't know until after the train left Denver. Ex-wife sent him a telegram and told him 'good luck.' Parents are divorced. Information we could get on the girl is in the files. I ain't read it."

Darby said, "I wonder if the outlaws even knew who she was when they took her? Or if they know now?"

"I don't know. That's for you to dig out. I'll lay it on the line. Allan was pissed about two of his agents going independent on him, so he told me not to give you any work until I had to."

"I wondered," Trace said. "Devious old fart."

"But when this came up, he sent a telegram. 'Get the blood hounds,' he said. I knew who he wanted. That's why I'm here."

Darby said, "So, what do you want us to do, and what will you pay?"

"Heard you was a lady that spoke her mind. Here's what Allan wants. He wants you to find the girl and bring her back if she's alive. You did something like that your last time out. Then he would like for you to find the gold and secure it someplace. Finally, he wants you to bring him the head of the snake."

"Head of the snake?" Darby asked.

"The man at the top of this gang. These aren't just a random bunch of outlaws that got together and took up robbing trains and banks. Everything's too well planned. And they always know when there's good money to be taken on a job. Allan thinks there's got to be somebody with inside information involved in these robberies."

"That's quite a load for only four of us," Darby said.

"If there are too many, word has a way of slipping out, but we'll have another ten agents on standby. A telegram will bring running as many as you need."

"Let's talk dollars," Darby said. "We'll take care of Clay's compensation. We'll treat him better than Pink would. Pinkerton's cheap."

Trace thought Darby's remark was the pot calling the kettle black.

"Well, Allan wired me a proposal. A four thousand-dollar advance. You pay your expenses out of that and keep the balance if you hit a dead end in a month's time."

"That's not worth crossing the street for," Darby complained. "It's an insult. We'd be better off advertising for our own clients."

"Now don't get on your high horse, Darby. I'm not done. It's the bonuses you want to listen to. Five thousand for recovery of the Sanford girl, dead or alive. Two percent of the value of any gold recovered."

Trace tensed. The bonus money was as much as the Crockett Agency could take in during a year scratching up routine protection work, probably more. Don't get greedy, Darby.

Darby said, "Take your bag back to Kansas City, Carl. If Allan thinks we're a bunch of chuckleheads, he wouldn't want us on the job. I'm guessing Pinkerton's in for twenty thousand on the girl and at least ten percent on the gold recovery. He's probably nailed down a base fee of at least twenty thousand."

"I offered what he told me to," Chirnside said, somewhat apologetically.

"But not what he authorized. Right?"

"Well, no."

Darby said, "Look, Carl. You don't know me, but Trace says you're a good guy."

Trace could not recall making such a statement. He did not dislike Carl, but he had no special affection for the man. He was a supervisor who did his job, which included resolving all doubts in favor of the boss. And Trace hoped Darby would not antagonize the man. Their financial survival was at stake in acquiring this assignment.

"I try to be fair," Chirnside said.

"Good," Darby said. "That's all we ask. So, we want eight thousand dollars for the advance. We could have a lot of expenses on this job. Ten thousand for the girl's return and five percent of the value of gold recovered."

"Maybe we could take a half percent off the gold and twenty-five hundred off the advance and the girl."

"You heard my final counter-offer, Carl. And we have sole authority to plan and carry out our strategies. You've contracted the job to us. No pre-approvals."

"I'll catch hell for this, but, yeah. I've got a contract with the other papers. I'll strike the control section and initial it. I just need to fill in some blanks on the money part."

Trace's head was spinning. If the assignment were a success, the detective agency and the ranch would have a lot of breathing room. He congratulated himself for his good judgment in marrying this woman. Even if they didn't earn the bonuses, the advance should make them solvent for a time. He did not underestimate their abilities, but the fees suggested there were dangers and difficulties that made the Crockett Agency critical to the task.

"Carl, the deal's made, but there's something you haven't told us. Why does Allan Pinkerton think we're so important for this job?" Trace asked.

"Well, I told you he wanted his blood hounds. He does think you and Darby are damned good operatives. But your last job took you to western Kansas and south to No Man's Land."

"Yeah, what's that go to do with it?"

"After the Blue Bandana Gang loaded the gold in a wagon at the wreck site, they headed south. The U. S. Marshal and his deputies lost the trail at the Cimarron River in No Man's Land. Found what was left of the wagon snagged on some washed-out trees a few miles downstream from where the trail disappeared."

"Our last trek out that way turned into a trip to hell. I'd have been glad not to ever go back," Trace said.

"I hope you have an easier trip this time," Chirnside said. "Oh, I forgot to mention another bonus hanging out there if you have some luck."

"What's that?"

"Five thousand dollars for the head of the snake." He looked at Darby. "Amount non-negotiable."

Chapter 7

AFTER CARL CHIRNSIDE departed, the four detectives sat at the conference table, each shuffling through a separate stack of papers taken from the manager's abandoned briefcase. Darby scanned a collection of newspaper articles about the tragic robbery, but what interested her most was a report by Pinkerton operatives who had investigated the scene. The notes indicated that the boxcar holding the bullion and, unfortunately, the detectives, had been blasted open by explosives and that the robbers had brought a wagon to haul the gold.

And yet another buckboard loaded with rock had been abandoned on the tracks. A passenger had seen four mules hitched to the wagon pulled up to the boxcar that carried the gold. The gang had come prepared, and the planners obviously had more than a clue regarding the content and size of the cargo. This was not a random strike.

She passed the ten-page report to Trace. "I think everyone should look at this report. This wasn't just a lucky strike. The leaders of this outfit knew what they were after. The gold was the target. Too many robbers for a routine job, too. But shipments like that aren't published in the newspaper. We need to find out who knew about the shipment and how they passed on the information."

Trace said, "I think we need to head to Denver and search out somebody that arranges the gold shipments. Then we see if they'll send another shipment of a hundred thousand dollars in bullion to the Mint. We'll guard the shipment coming east. We've got to draw the Blue Bandana Gang out. We'll never find them on a cold trail."

"Pinkerton and the Santa Fe won't want to risk another gold loss," Darby pointed out.

Trace was silent, but she could sense he was on to something. Finally, he said, "The gold doesn't get loaded. Our Denver agents will pick it up at the station and take it someplace for safekeeping. We travel with an empty boxcar, except for the Gatling gun."

"Gatling gun? What are you talking about?"

"Charlie over at the Chuckwagon. He's got a Gatling gun for sale. He said not to ask where he got it, but he thought that, as an old Army sergeant, I might be interested. This thing's outdated, but he says it works, and he's got ammunition, a few belts . . . the works. He wants fifty dollars, but you can probably get it for half. Turn on the charm and the cheap."

"You'd see charm if we didn't have our friends present."

She considered his suggestion. Maybe he was on to something. She had no doubt Trace could handle the weapon. He had served in the Red River War fighting Comanche and had been a few months from West Point graduation when he was forced to resign as the result of a romantic relationship with a Colonel's wife. "We'd have to load the gun on the train and haul it to Denver."

"I've figured that out. We box it in a coffin. Store it at the Denver terminal, then put it in the gold car when we get ready to leave. Nobody would be interested in opening a coffin if the robbers have somebody watching the depot."

Clay Sibley spoke for the first time. "I could build two identical coffins. One would be for the gold. We have the gold placed in the coffin and hauled to the station. Then we make a switch some way."

"I like that idea, Clay. You're a carpenter?" Trace asked.

"I've done a fair amount along the way. If I have the lumber and tools, I can turn out a few passable coffins in a half day."

Audra seemed distracted by the silver Pinkerton badge and credentials Carl Chirnside had given her just before he departed. She still clutched the badge and documents in her hand as she studied the papers. Darby supposed that the former prostitute saw the moment as tangible evidence of her step up to respectability. Sometimes Darby saw a child in Audra, though the young woman was only a couple years younger than her own twenty-five. It seemed that Audra needed periodic reassurance from her peers, though she was wise beyond her years in the ways of the world and had earned her place in the firm.

Audra looked up. "The Wheaton mansion has a wonderful wood shop attached to the stable and every tool you can imagine. If we can get the lumber delivered there, I'm sure Elisabeth would be glad to have Clay use it. I don't have to ask, but I will. I'm positive he can lodge in one of the rooms there, too. That way, he can leave anything behind he doesn't need in Denver."

Clay turned to her. "Who is this Elisabeth?"

Audra said, "Elisabeth Denney. She's trustee of all of the assets owned by Miranda Wheaton, the Wheaton heir. The Wheaton family owns and operates ranch lands, limestone quarries and kilns, as well as the Wheaton Inn, which you would have passed on your way to the office. I lodge in the house temporarily. She is a great Pinkerton friend."

"But how would she feel about you dragging home a colored man to board in her house?"

Audra giggled. "Trust me on that."

Darby's initial impression of Clayton Sibley was that he was a reserved, somewhat shy, man. Audra would be his opposite, and each might find the other a bit of a challenge at the beginning. Her bet was that Audra would find a way to tug the unsuspecting man from his shell.

Trace finished scanning the Pinkerton report and passed it on to Clay. "The gold is shipped from the Denver branch of the Philadelphia Mint, it appears. We need to have the Philadelphia office order a shipment, or the wrong guy might figure out we're trying to set something up."

Darby said, "I'll send a wire to Chicago. I'm sure Pink can arrange it. As you know, I worked out of the Denver office before a 'wanna-be' cowboy came along and changed my life. I know the folks there, so we can work out the details on that end after we get there."

Audra said, "I wonder if somebody should talk to Maddie Sanford's mother when we get to Denver. According to a story on the society page in The Rocky Mountain News, an Alexandra Sanford lives in Denver. Chairwoman of the Denver Indian Orphanage. She's mentioned in a story about a charity ball for her cause. The name was underlined by one of the investigators, so I assume that this was a message to connect us to the mother."

Darby said, "Why don't you take on that task? It might help us to know something about the girl. If she's alive, that could be important."

"I'll do that."

Trace said, "We haven't really set out the plan, but I think everybody can see where we're going. We're going to try to bring the outlaws to us instead of hitting a cold trail. We'll take the train back from Denver with another load of gold bullion . . . smaller this time, because it would stand to reason the government would be wary about a larger shipment given what happened earlier. We won't have the gold, but we hope to intercept the Blue Bandana Gang. Ideally, we take a live prisoner or two and get them to talk about the hideout location. Otherwise, we've got a warm trail. I'd like to load our own horses for the trip."

Trace turned to Clay. "You were cavalry, so I guess time on horseback won't be a problem."

"I've been on horseback since I wasn't more than a sprout. Did a lot of hunting from the back of a horse."

"We've got extra horses out at our place. You can look them over in the morning and see if one suits you."

Darby said, "Trace, you'll need to be in the boxcar with the Gatling gun. I'll be there with you. Clay and Audra, you'll be with the passenger cars. We'll place Audra as a passenger. And Clay . . ." she hesitated.

Clay said, "I should be serving in the Pullman dining car, if they have one. Otherwise, I could be a porter. A Negro in those positions wouldn't be noticed by anybody. Don't be uncomfortable. There's a reason Pinkerton hires colored men and women, and I understand. I'm fine with that. My skin got me a decent job."

Darby nodded. "I'd like to leave day after tomorrow. I'll check about tickets and reservations. I think we can ride together on the way to Denver. I'll see if there is a compartment where we can have privacy to discuss the case."

Chapter 8

WHILE THE OTHERS continued review of the Pinkerton reports and documents, Audra stepped next door to speak with Suzanne. She was greeted by the laughter of the occupants, who were apparently enjoying each other's company while they painted the room. Suzy and Jimmy, a budding romance? Why not? They were about the same age, a few years younger than herself, ambitious and hard-working. They could end up a good team, she thought.

Flaxen-haired Suzanne was a bubbly, happy sort who seemed unaware of the wholesome beauty and vibrant personality that likely played no small part in bringing the parade of men of all ages to her new barbershop. Jimmy, at first glance, was more of a scruffy string bean, but his lively translucent, blue eyes, would catch any woman's attention. He had a charming smile and just might clean up nicely, Audra decided.

Even after she closed the door, the pair had not noticed her, and Suzanne, who was on her knees painting woodwork, started when Audra spoke. "Suzy, are you going back to the house soon?"

Suzanne put her paint can and brush aside and stood up. "Yeah, we're about finished here. We'll clean up and get my chairs and furniture in place, and then I'm taking Jimmy to the house to look at a repair project Elisabeth wants him to bid on."

"Would you tell Elisabeth that I won't return until after supper? The firm's going to meet over supper at the Chuck Wagon."

"I'll tell her to set one less place."

"And tell her I'll be bringing an overnight guest, a Pinkerton detective, if she doesn't mind putting him in one of the spare rooms. If she'd rather not, perhaps you could send the stable boy to tell me to make other arrangements."

Suzanne laughed, "She's still treating us like royalty for bringing Miranda Wheaton home. You could bring a pack of wolves to the mansion, and she'd find accommodations for them."

Later, Audra picked up the horse and buggy at the livery stable and reined up in front of the Crockett office so Clay could load his bags. He appeared to travel light, but she noticed a heavier canvas bag that obviously carried weapons. Interesting, she thought, that Trace never left his personal arsenal behind either. Clay was obviously no stranger to guns. The new operative had spoken little of his personal history, revealing fragments of his past only when he couldn't avoid it, and she did not fault him for that. She was not ready to tell him, either, that she had once been a high-class prostitute.

When Clay climbed into the buggy beside her, he said, "I still feel uneasy about this, going to some strange woman's house and expecting her to take me in overnight. If she runs the hotel, wouldn't she rather I pay a night's lodging there?"

"No. Elisabeth Denney would never think of it that way. If you're a friend of mine and Trace and Darby's, she would be offended if you didn't stay with her. She refuses to allow Suzanne and me to leave until we've found the perfect place. Frankly, I don't argue with her much. It's about as close to a home as I've ever had."

Audra tugged the reins and then relaxed them, signaling the mare to move out.

"She sounds like an interesting and kind woman. Running these companies, taking on guardianship of a child."

"She is both. It's a long story, but she worked for the companies' founder, Congrave Wheaton, as his personal assistant for some years before he died. She inherited a sizable share of the companies, but the majority interest will go to his granddaughter, Miranda, when she's thirty-five. That's seventeen or eighteen years from now. Until then, Elisabeth controls everything. Her job is to prepare Miranda for managing the inheritance."

"It all sounds very complicated."

"For now, I'll just say that without the Pinkerton Detective Agency, Miranda would never have been found and given this opportunity. But in a matter of a few months, the girl has come to love Elisabeth. They're like mother and daughter, and I think they both realize how lucky they are to have each other."

"Well, I've certainly been placed in an unusual situation here. I hope I can prove my worth on this job. I seem to get one surprise after another."

"What do you mean?"

"I couldn't believe it when Darby said I would be paid twenty percent above my regular Pinkerton salary regardless of outcome. And then she said I would get a ten percent cut of any bonus money. And Trace didn't bat an eye. I know she hadn't asked him."

"Trace trusts her totally, and she knows it. They trust each other. She'll have his back, too, even if she disagrees with him. We all have each other's back, and we'll have yours, too. Count on it."

"I like this town. I'm nervous when I go to restaurants. I've been turned down places. Nobody seemed to pay any attention at the Chuck Wagon. And there was a colored couple there."

Audra said, "The town was founded by Free Staters who moved here to keep Kansas a non-slave state before the Civil War—that's how Darby explained it to me. There is a place or two you might be turned away, and there are a few folks who might not treat you kindly, but you aren't likely to run into trouble here. Negroes and white kids, and all kinds of mixed bloods, go to the same schools. Of course, if I can put it bluntly, you could pass for Indian, maybe even Mexican, if you wanted. Might need to keep your hat on, though."

He chuckled, "I like that kind of bluntness. I don't like dancing around this race stuff. You said we could be related. You must have Cherokee blood."

"On my mother's side. I'm quarter blood."

"I'm half. My father was a runaway slave who ended up with the Cherokee, and, to look at him, you could tell the African had been watered down by a few slave owners in the lineage. Strange, always thought of their Negroes as livestock, just animals. But I don't suppose most took up fornication with their cows and pigs."

"You must have gone to one of the Quaker schools on Cherokee lands."

"Yeah. I was lucky. I got a good education through eighth grade in Arkansas before the war broke out. The teacher at the school there arranged a scholarship for me to go to a Quaker boarding school in Pennsylvania for high school, and my folks headed into Indian Territory to wait out the war. I didn't appreciate it at the time, but that teacher gave me a rare opportunity."

"My formal schooling ended when I finished eighth grade. Not long after my pa decided to uproot the family and head west. That's when I got a different kind of education."

She turned the mare through an open gate and up a drive paved with crushed limestone. When she reined the buggy to a stop in front of the wide, railed veranda, a young man appeared from behind the house.

"Good evening, Miss Scott. I'll put up the horse and buggy but let me help you unload."

"Thank you, Jake." She noticed that Clay grabbed his gun bag but let Jake take the carpet bag and leather valise and set them in front of the door. The young liveryman disappeared quickly.

Audra saw that a wide-eyed Clay Sibley was casting his eyes over the limestone walls of the enormous house. "See why there's room for another guest?" she asked.

"You didn't say I'd be staying in a castle."

"Folks around here call it 'Wheaton Manor.'"

One of the double doors opened, and a soft, orange glow dropped over their faces. A tall, dusky woman with thick sable hair falling to a few inches above her shoulders, stepped into the doorway. Clay removed his hat, and the woman's dark eyes seemed to give him a quick study. The perusal did not surprise Audra. Clay cut a very striking figure, and, although she did not betray surprise, the exotically attractive woman, most certainly would have noted the appearance of a man, who, like herself, carried the blood of African ancestors.

"Audra, introduce your colleague and show him in," Elisabeth Denney said.

Chapter 9

MADDIE SANFORD HAD spent more than a week isolated from the other occupants of a place she understood to be Copperhead Canyon. She could not say how long she had resided in the musty single-room, mud-caulked log cabin. She had lost count at five days, and she thought her stay was at least three or four days beyond that.

She spent days and nights on a bug-infested buffalo robe that covered part of the cabin's dirt floor. The thing smelled of cat piss but not like the urine of a barn cat like those half-wild creatures that hunted the rats and mice at the family ranch. No, this would have been a big devil, a cougar, probably. She worried that the odor might attract a relative. She welcomed the robe's warmth at night, though, and was not about to give it up. She suspected that it was the source of the angry red welts that were devouring her flesh, however.

Perhaps the cougar had killed a past user of the robe and then, in contempt, pissed on the thing before dragging off the victim. She wished she had the fixings for a cigarette. It would calm her, and the aroma might crowd out some of the cat piss smell.

Thinking of the rancid buffalo robe reminded her that she needed to pee. She hated to ask the guard, who was posted by a tree some forty feet from the front entrance of the windowless building. After she had peed her pants the second day of captivity in the canyon abode, the man called Corker agreed to let her out to take care of necessaries so long as a guard accompanied her. That wouldn't have been so bad, but one of the guards often stood within five feet when she dropped her britches and relieved herself.

And she had no undergarments now. After wetting her underpants, somebody had disposed of the things. She guessed it didn't matter since she wasn't allowed to launder anyway. She had just hung up the wet britches on the door till they dried. She was not taken anywhere to bathe, either. She knew she stank. She had been wearing the same baggy flannel shirt and tattered denims since her arrival, the now-dry trousers secured about her waist with a rope. She was shoeless, she supposed to further discourage her escape.

The gunnysack that served as her cabin door was tugged aside, and Maddie was glad to see that the visitor was Minnie, the nearest thing she had to a friend in this hellhole. She knew there were other women in the little colony, but Minnie appeared to be her caretaker. She was a mulatto woman, boney but not in a sickly way, hair shorn to just below her ears. Practical for the way they lived here, Maddie thought. Maybe she would ask Minnie to cut the tangled nest her hair had become.

"Maddie, how are y'all this afternoon?" Minnie asked, her voice reflecting the accent of her native New Orleans. Minnie's tentative smile always cheered her some, but it belied the woman's perpetually sad eyes. She was not quite pretty, but Maddie thought the tawny-skinned woman could be, carrying a few extra pounds of flesh in the right places and exhibiting a happier face.

"Can you take me out to pee? That Mexican guard won't take his eyes off my ass when I drop my britches. Filthy as I am, he'd take me in a minute if he got a chance."

"I'll go with y'all and try to keep him back a ways, but I ain't got any right to stop him. Order is to leave you be so long as y'all be good and don't cause no trouble. For now, anyhow."

She followed Minnie outside, and they went behind the cabin. Some of the cabins had crude privies, but this one did not. There was a little clearing amidst some trees twenty feet from the cabin where previous occupants had also relieved bowels and bladders. The blistering afternoon sun seemed to stir up the stench, but Maddie found her nostrils were achieving some immunity by now. She looked over her shoulder to confirm the guard had not followed—they usually kept their distance when Minnie chaperoned. Then, she untied the rope ends that kept her britches up and took care of business.

When they returned to the cabin, they sat down on the ground in front of the entryway and bathed in the sun's warm rays. The guards generally cut some slack when Minnie was with her, and Maddie snatched every opportunity to escape the cabin's darkness. More importantly she wanted to survey the lay of the land. She didn't intend to stay much longer—a few days, maybe.

"Minnie, could you cut my hair? Short, like yours."

The dark woman looked at Maddie, appraising her with her soulful eyes. "I could do that easy enough. Couldn't make it look any worser. Bring my shears when I come with supper."

After Maddie had wet her pants, Minnie had been charged with feeding Maddie and checking on the captive from time to time, and Maddie figured she had been lucky on that score. The mulatto woman was a more than competent cook, and the outlaw hideout seemed to carry an ample supply of foodstuffs. The two had formed a bond that Maddie could not yet define, but Maddie sensed they were approaching trust now. She had been wary of Minnie at first, thinking she might be a spy for her captors, but increasingly she wondered if Minnie lived in the "roost," as the colored woman called it, by choice.

Minnie was obviously uneducated in the things people attached to knowledge. She had mentioned to Maddie several days earlier that she did not know her letters or numbers, and she had spoken of this with apparent sadness. But Maddie's father had mentioned once that many folks had acquired formal education beyond their intelligence. He had cautioned her not to judge people by scholarly achievement. There were different kinds of knowledge, he insisted, much of it not found in books. She suspected Minnie's intelligence was far ahead of her formal education. She knew things a person would not learn in school.

Maddie decided to take a chance with Minnie. "Do you like it here, Minnie?"

Minnie cocked her head to one side and looked at Maddie, one eye squinting as if wondering whether she had been the recipient of a trick question. "Course not. I'm a prisoner in Copperhead Canyon. Not like you, maybe. But just as much."

"I don't understand."

"Bull Killer found me in Kansas City. I had my own crib there."

"Crib?"

"Room where I spread my legs for a poke. Lotsa white men pay extra for a Nigger poke. Don't know why. Whorin' was all I knowed. Mama was a whore, and I was raised in a whorehouse in New Orleans till I joined up in the business. Anyhow, Bull Killer like what I give him and say he make me rich if I go to No Man's Land with him. Figured the way I was going, I didn't have no more than five years left in the business—customers like the young, fresh ones—so gettin' rich didn't sound so bad. I come here with Bull Killer. Then I find trouble. He got Smoke Brown shacked up here."

"So you had two men to take care of, so to speak?"

"Cook for, keep house for two men. Turns out, only one to take pokes from . . . sometimes."

"But the three of you live together. Looks from here like a one-room cabin, a little bigger than mine, maybe."

"It be like this. Smoke, he queer. Know what that is?"

"I've heard whispers about it. He likes men for sex?"

"You got it, missy. And Bull Killer like both. Man or woman. Makes him no difference."

"That does sound like a problem."

"I don't care what they does. I got my own feather mattress on the floor across the room, and they got the bed. They fool around, and my blanket goes over my head, and I try not to hear what's happening. But sometimes Bull Killer come to me for a poke. That okay, but Smoke don't like that, and they fight and cuss about it. Smoke beat the hell out of me, like it was my idea. And I been here a year and ain't got a penny for it."

"Have you tried to leave?"

"I say I want to go, and Bull say he have to kill me first. See, most men don't want nothing to do with queers. Okay to share a woman. But man on man. No good to others. Can't let nobody know. They could get killed for it. Bull say I make them . . . don't know the word."

"Respectable?"

"Yeah. That sound right. Anyway, I try to go away, I'se dead. Know too much. Like y'all. Don't like to say it, Sweets, but they ain't letting us out of this canyon alive. Neither of us. I hear Bull Killer and Smoke talk. They pay no attention to me. They holding y'all as hostage if trouble comes. Say y'alls daddy pay big money for you. But he never get y'all back. Big boss try to figure out how to get money and keep you."

"I thought it was something like that. That Corker checks on me every few days. He seems really nervous about me. One day he brought an important-looking man with him—Bart, I think his name was."

"That be Bart Wince. He's little boss. Big boss don't come here." Minnie clambered to her feet. "I got to go. If Smoke or Bull need something and don't find me there, I likely get the shit beat out of me. They get money for feeding y'all, so don't care about that, but hell to pay if I take too long. I feed them first. Tonight, they go to Gimpy's cabin to play poker. Be gone till sun almost comes up. Both will be staggering drunk, and Smoke mean as a grizzly. But tonight, I'll have time to cut y'alls hair. Talk some, maybe."

"Yes, we'll definitely talk."

Chapter 10

MADDIE DECIDED TO risk telling Minnie of her plan to escape. She was confident her friend would not reveal her intent, and there was a possibility the woman would want to join her. She should at least have the opportunity.

Maddie found herself impatient as she sat alone in the darkness, waiting for suppertime. As the afternoon wore on, she got up from the buffalo robe and went to the entryway repeatedly, pulling back the burlap bag and peering out for some sign of Minnie's approach. The cabin where she lived with Smoke and Bull Killer was across a draw to the north not more than fifty yards distant. The cabins were scattered all about the canyon floor, hers on low shale-covered ground, but many were perched on hillocks and knolls above the gulches and gullies that carved the floor like giant spider webs. She wondered if the high-ground cabins had been located to avoid the floods that rushed through the canyon during torrential rains. Perhaps that accounted for the dampness of her floor and the suffocating musty smell when the sun was highest.

Finally, she peeked out and saw Minnie, carrying several full bags, moving quickly, despite the burden, along the trail toward the cabin. Graceful and fast, like an antelope. Her long legs, slender but muscle-sheathed, were revealed by the ragged garment that fell not quite to her knees and was more breechclout than skirt. Maddie tossed a glance toward the guard standing under the towering cottonwood tree in front of the cabin. His eyes were fixed on Minnie, and Maddie figured she could slip out and dart around the cabin, and he would never notice. She knew what was doing that man's thinking right now, and it wasn't his brain.

Wally had got that way, too—most of the time when she was with him, it seemed. Not that she begrudged him. She had learned a lot and had some good times with that nineteen-year-old cowboy. He was on the dim-witted side, but she loved the smoking and drinking and laughing they did together, and, of course, the humping. She liked most of all that their dalliance drove her mother crazy. She hated that Wally was dead. She had not loved him, at least not the way she thought romantic love was supposed to be. But he had a special place in her head, if not in her heart. He would always be her first, but she knew he would not be her only, not if she lived through this. She despised her mother for having Wally killed. Thank God, Wally had not gotten her with child. It was not for lack of planting the seeds that she had escaped that complication.

When Minnie ducked through the entryway, she set her bags on the floor, pulled a short rope from the dirty canvas bag and half-hitched it about the burlap door cover and bunched it up to let in some light. Then she opened the poplin sack and removed a pair of moccasins and tossed them to Maddie. "Been workin' on these. Should fit."

Maddie snatched the moccasins up and slipped them on her feet. "Perfect. Thank you so much."

Then Minnie took out a tin plate wrapped with burlap and took off the cover. She handed the plate to Maddie along with a fork. Minnie offered a canteen, but Maddie's was half full yet, and she plucked it off the floor and dropped it in her lap. The plate was heaped full. Beans, fried potatoes, rib meat and two biscuits.

"Them's venison ribs," Minnie said. "Them two pigs I feed over there et up all the cobbler I made up. Got no sweets for y'all."

"This will be plenty, Minnie. I have no complaints about the grub I've had since I got here."

"I got more ribs wrapped up in this bag, and biscuits, too. Maybe good for two days. That all."

"Why? Aren't you going to keep bringing meals?"

"We ain't going to be here, Sweets. We getting our asses out."

"You'll really go with me?"

"Won't stay no more. Maybe we help one another."

"I was hoping you'd go with me. But tonight?"

"Best for me, with Smoke and Bull over at Gimpy's. Best for y'all."

"What's that got to do with it?"

"Heard the men talkin'. There ain't gonna be no ransom, Sweets. Too risky. They got no need for y'all no more. Bart come a few days back about 'nother train job, then go to see big boss again. Get final okay. Gets back, it be all done for you."

Minnie was as much as saying a death sentence had been rendered. It was just a matter of when and how they carried it out. "You're right. I've got to go, and I'd welcome your company if you really want to do this."

"As much for me as for y'all, Sweets. Don't want to wait around for the axe to come down on my turkey neck. But y'all eat now. Then, I get them ole shears and take that nest off y'alls head. We ain't leavin' till it' coal-black dark out there."

Maddie started forking the beans and potatoes in her mouth. "What about the guard?"

"Can y'all shoot one of them rifles?"

"I'm better than good, if I say so myself."

"Can't shoot the big gun but can trigger a six-gun close up. Killed me some men that needed killin' but mostly use knife."

"But what does this have to do with the guard?"

"He gots guns. We need guns. So us two, we take the guns. Eat. I cut y'alls hair. Then we gets the guns. I brung good news, too."

"What's that?" Maddie asked.

"Gang short of help here. Bax Corker ride out on job today. Took Jim-Bob, Stick and Pete along and some gunners from other crew."

"Moon Parker, too? I hate him."

"Nope. Bax don't like him. Leave Gimp, Smoke and Bull to keep their eyes after you." She laughed. "Like chickens lookin' after foxes. We's the foxes. And Moon Parker, he some relations to Bart. Him's and Shales—other crew boss—watching over gold. Bart gone again and be back to take gold out soons Bax come back with more."

"But there must still be ten or more men left behind."

"Not twenty anyhow."

Shortly before sunset, Minnie finished shearing Maddie's hair. The young woman raked her fingers through her scalp and down her neck. The feeling of close-cropped hair was foreign to her, since for as long as she could remember her hair had been at least shoulder length, but it brightened her mood to be rid of the tangled and knotted mat.

"I wish I had a mirror," Maddie said.

"No. No, y'all don't want that. But this be okay. Now, we get guns."

"How?"

"Feel blades." Minnie thrust the shears toward Maddie.

The girl took the big scissors in her hand, running her fingers tentatively over the cutting blades. "Razor-sharp." She meant that literally. The blades were finely honed, as keen-edged as her father's shaving instrument.

"Now, see this." Minnie took the shears back, wedged her thumbnail into the groove of the screw that joined the blades and commenced turning. The blades separated, and the mulatto handed one of the oval-handled blades to Maddie. "Knife for y'all and knife for me."

With dusk, Minnie's form was shadowy now, but Maddie could see the perfect white teeth that formed a wicked smile. She realized at that moment that the prostitute had not been joshing her about her ability to kill a man. It was not just luck that Minnie had survived a life that to most women would have been unbearable.

"We're going to use these, aren't we?"

"Yes, ma'am. I is, anyways. Put y'alls blade in the rope-belt just over your ass, like me. Then, y'all come along and walk behind me about five steps back. Stay back lessen I say 'help.' Y'all should see how this be done, but don't want y'all in the fuss if don't have to."

Maddie found her fingers trembling as she positioned the blade. If she understood the crazy woman correctly, Minnie planned to kill the guard. It was confirmed when Minnie waved for her to follow and slipped through the cabin opening. Obediently, she fell in behind.

Minnie headed straight for the sentry, who had been leaning against the tree when he spotted her. He straightened, cradled his rifle in his arms and took a few steps toward the approaching visitors.

"Hold up, gals. Where the hell do you think you're headed?"

Maddie had not been up close to the man before. He had not been with the crew that had taken her captive. He wore a battered Stetson, a nondescript shirt, and britches that were too snug to contain a pot belly. Squirrel-like cheeks, perhaps with tobacco chaw secreted there, were covered by a week's growth of whiskers.

"I come to talk to y'all, Hank." She tugged the top of her frayed shirt down to reveal the beginnings of taut, nicely formed breasts.

"This ain't a social gathering, Minnie. Go away."

"Half dollar and y'all can poke me."

He lifted his brow, and his eyes roamed her body.

"Got a dollar gold piece. What I get for that?"

"What y'all wants?"

Maddie could see the man was struggling. He was suspicious, but he wanted Minnie in the worst way.

"Send the girl away. Don't want her watchin'."

"Maybe her play, too. Y'all don't wants her to sneak off. She stay back but where y'all can see her."

Minnie stepped closer, moving slowly, seductively. She lifted her ragged skirt, exposing herself, and Hank licked his lips. He clung to his rifle, but his thoughts weren't with the weapon when Minnie reached him, placed her fingers on the front of his britches and began to unbutton the front. Then her right hand eased behind her back and clutched the blade, swinging it around in a single sweep, driving the point into the man's soft belly and yanking it upward. He grunted and opened his mouth to scream, but the sound did not follow. He dropped his rifle and his knees buckled and he tumbled over. Minnie knelt and began unbuckling the man's gun belt.

Maddie joined her and picked up the rifle. "Any cartridges . . . bullets in his pocket?"

Minnie rummaged through the trouser pockets. "Two gold pieces. Little knife." She handed the items to Maddie, and she dropped the penknife and gold pieces in her front pocket. The rifle was a Winchester, but she wasn't sure how to tell one pistol from another. Some used the same size cartridge as compatible rifles. Anyway, there should be fifteen or sixteen cartridges in the rifle if she remembered correctly.

They drug the guard's body away and rolled it into a nearby ravine, thinking that with the darkness he might not be discovered until morning. Minnie headed back to the cabin with the cartridge belt and holstered pistol in hand, and Maddie followed with the Winchester. Maddie looked skyward. She could not be certain of the time but thought it had been no more than an hour since sundown. She had watched guard changes during her captivity and thought they came much later—or hoped that was the case. She guessed they would have three to five hours head start.

Minnie reached into her canvas bag and pulled out a short rope. "Roll up the buffalo hide. Make a toting loop. Y'all carry the robe and rifle. I bring my bag." While she spoke, she was stuffing the food and canteens into the canvas bag, which apparently contained whatever Minnie considered vital to their journey.

Maddie said, "They'll expect us to head downstream to the canyon's mouth. The stream comes from someplace. They said this is a blind canyon, but is there a way out the back?"

"No wagon road, but I seen men walk out and in from that way. Fishin' up there, I think."

"I can see the stream from here. We should go there and follow it west."

"Okay. I ain't much carin.' I wants to run, die free anyways."

Chapter 11

AUDRA SCOTT WAS surprised to learn that Alexandra Sanford, Maddie's mother, resided in the Denver Castle, a luxurious hotel with a main floor of residential suites. Audra, attired in conservative business jacket and skirt, stopped at the front desk and informed the young male clerk she would like to visit Mrs. Sanford. He brushed a mop of red hair back from his forehead and studied her suspiciously, before looking at a book spread out on the counter.

"I don't see any appointments for Mrs. Sanford this morning."

Audra plucked her Pinkerton badge from her bag and pushed it toward the clerk, enjoying the heady feeling of the first display of her operative's authorization, realizing it carried no powers of compulsion. "Perhaps you could tell Mrs. Sanford I'm here about her daughter."

The clerk picked up the badge, glanced at it and handed it back. "I'll see if she's available."

Ten minutes later, Audra was seated in the elegant sitting room of the Sanford suite with an attractive, albeit somewhat Rubenesque, woman with long, chestnut-colored hair and a face that make-up had rendered almost sickly pale.

"Thank you for seeing me, Mrs. Sanford. I'm with a group of Pinkerton operatives, who have been dispatched to recover your daughter. I thought it might be useful for us to know a bit about Maddie, obtain some idea about how she might react to her abduction."

"You're talking to the wrong person. The last few years, I've only seen her bitchy side. She was always her father's daughter. Before the divorce a year ago, we lived on a ranch just outside Denver—I hated it there and got away from the hellhole every chance I got. Maddie loved the place. Tom—my ex-husband, spoiled her rotten, turned her into a cowgirl. She's crazy about horses, hunts rabbits and deer, ropes calves and helps with branding. Tom was gone a lot with railroad business, so the other cowhands more or less adopted her. Then she met this young cowboy and turned into a smoking, drinking slut. Six months ago, we moved into the hotel, but I couldn't keep her here. She kept riding out to the ranch. Refused to come back until I came out with a sheriff's deputy to bring her back. Fortunately, the cowboy lover met with a shooting accident, and after his death she wasn't so interested in the trips to the ranch. She agreed to stay put when I stabled her two favorite horses in town."

Audra asked, "Where was her father during this time?"

"Kansas City. He's worked out of that office since he's taken up with some sweet, young thing there. She claims to be a schoolteacher, but she's no better than a whore. She's after his money, of course."

Audra flinched at the reference to her former occupation but supposed she would become accustomed to it someday. "As I understand it, the day of the abduction, Maddie was travelling to Kansas City to visit her father."

Alexandra Sanford's lips curled into a snarl. "Ha. She was going to live with her father—at my insistence. I'd had enough of her sneaking out, meeting up with boys and drinking, and I can only imagine what else. We were at constant war, and I'd had enough of her dirty mouth. She blamed me for the divorce. Well, I did file. Incompatibility. After a few years, Tom's charm wore off, and I learned I had to make my own life if I wanted one. We just gave up on each other, I suppose. I get some satisfaction that the ranch is up for sale, so he can pay me out and hang onto the rest of his damned railroad holdings, although his lawyer contacted mine a few weeks back about me taking the railroad stock in settlement. He loved that ranch. Maybe he wants to go broke being a cowboy. Either way, I'll be fixed moneywise."

Audra tried to keep the woman on the subject. "So, Maddie was going to live with her father. How were these arrangements made? Is there anyone who would have known she was making the trip? Especially someone who would have had time to plan a kidnapping?"

"I don't see how. It was spur of the moment. I purchased a ticket the afternoon before. That night, I told Maddie I was giving her what she wanted. She was going to go live with her father, and she should pack her things. I put her on the train early the next morning. Later, I telegraphed Tom that his daughter was on the way and that he should meet her at the depot."

Her statement was consistent with Pinkerton reports. "Our last word was that there had been no ransom demand. You haven't received any demand, I assume?"

"No, they might be about ready to pay somebody to take her back."

Audra thought the woman's statement was despicable at a time like this, but people under duress did not always react normally. Inside, her turmoil and grief might be overwhelming. On the other hand, her own widowed father had abandoned Audra in Dodge City when she was about Maddie's age after catching his daughter naked with one of the wagon train boys she had taken up with. She could not help identifying with the girl and decided that the mother had little to offer other than more venom.

Chapter 12

TRACE WAS NOT impressed with the Philadelphia Mint's Denver office. There was talk that someday Denver would host a full-fledged mint in its own right given accessibility to the raw materials for gold and silver coinage, but he supposed the West did not yet harvest enough votes for politicians to make that a reality any time soon. For now, a single-room office with ten desks and chairs and half the occupants staring blankly out a large front window served as a conduit for gold and silver shipped to the Philadelphia Mint for coinage.

The office, with its separate entrance, was located in the Colorado Continental Bank building, a new brick structure, and he supposed accessibility to the institution's vaults had been a placement factor. There were no private offices, and Trace and Darby were meeting with Horace Youngblood, a thin, narrow-shouldered man with a receding hairline, who had introduced himself as the Denver Director. His territory was distinguished by two, rather than one, visitor chairs and a bit more space between his work area and that of the others in the cramped room. Still, three or four men—they were all males—were within convenient listening distance.

Trace presented Darby and himself, and they each produced their Pinkerton badges as they sat down. Youngblood, a fifty-ish man, Trace thought, seemed to be giving careful attention to the badges, but Trace suspected the man was exhibiting his own self-importance in making the meaningless examination.

Youngblood rubbed his clean-shaven face thoughtfully and said, "Husband and wife agents? That's a new one. Well, nothing to me. What's your business here?"

Trace said, "Three hundred one-pound gold bars. Close to a hundred thousand dollars."

"I see. You know about the order from Philadelphia then?"

"Yes," Trace said. "Your home office contacted the Pinkerton Chicago office for shipment protection. Chicago notified Denver, and Darby and I were given the assignment."

"Pinkertons didn't do so good last time out. Lost a woman and a man. All do respect, ma'am. That was no place for a woman."

Trace worried that Darby would get up and break the man's nose, but she remained admirably silent.

Youngblood summoned the man at the next desk some five feet distant. "Orval, step over here a minute, will you?"

Trace guessed that the man, stoop-shouldered and paunchy with a green-tinted eyeshade perched on a bald scalp, was about Youngblood's age, but he could pass for a dozen years older. His flaccid form and pale complexion attested to a life spent behind a desk. "What is it, Horace?" The man's voice was high-pitched to the point of being cringeworthy.

Youngblood said, "This is the Assistant Denver Director, Orval Dirks. He will make any arrangements, so he needs to hear what you have got to say. Orval, this is Mister and Missus Crockett. They're Pinkertons assigned to guard the new shipment we got the telegram about."

"I see," Dirks squeaked. "The smelter's pouring the bars. We should have the shipment in the bank vault here day after tomorrow."

"That'll be fine," Trace said. "Can we ship them out the morning after? Atchison, Topeka & Santa Fe to Kansas City. Somebody will relieve us there."

"I don't see why not."

"We'll check back with you on time and details. I assume you are confident you don't have any security leaks here. I'm nervous as a hen at a coyote meeting about this. Those were top operatives guarding during that last heist. I complained we needed more people, but Pinkerton squeezes that dollar damned tight."

Youngblood said, "I'll guarantee our security. Too many losses, and Philly looks for another source, and our jobs are gone. Everybody knows that."

"Well, we'll do our best, but my wife and I won't be dying for this. If that Blue Bandana bunch or anybody else shows up, we'll only go so far before we drop the gold overboard." Trace stood, and Darby joined him. "We'll check back day after tomorrow to confirm delivery arrangements to the station."

Outside, as they walked away, Darby said, "I don't trust either of those men. They're a pair of snakes."

"You don't trust anybody."

"In our business, that's an asset. I love you, Trace, but sometimes you're too trusting of people."

"I don't think that's true. I'm just inclined to hold off judgment for a spell, just like I did with you."

"What do you mean by that?"

"Well, when we first met up, I wasn't sure about you. That pretty blonde lady I met at lawyer Locke's office? I didn't think I wanted to work with her. But she didn't turn out so bad."

"Didn't turn out so bad?"

"Yeah, she was a regular demon in bed. Not a bad detective, either."

She gave him an elbow in the ribs.

Chapter 13

TWO DAYS LATER, Trace and Darby stopped by the Pinkerton Denver headquarters mid-afternoon to confirm plans with the manager, Jack Winslow, and his assistant, Newton Cromwell. Darby had been attached to the Denver office when she met Trace on an assignment and knew and trusted Winslow, an easy-going, craggy-faced man with twinkling sky-blue eyes. He had been with Pinkerton during the Civil War years. She knew Winslow to be an excellent detective, but she thought he was a bit lax as a manager. She considered the office overstaffed and was surprised Allan Pinkerton did not question the payroll costs. Most of the workload was for the railroads, however, and the companies were lucrative enterprises these days, so their budget for the premier, if not only, national detective firm was probably not closely scrutinized.

Darby knew Cromwell from her previous service in Denver, but she had reported directly to Winslow and spent most of her time out of the office on assignments. Her acquaintance with the man was only casual. She guessed he was in his mid-thirties, some twenty years younger than his superior. Thick, brown hair, serious gray eyes, average height, he was a man who would not be noticed in a crowd, an attribute for a detective. His manner of speech suggested an educated background, and his responses to questions were generally brief and pointed. Could he be trusted and depended upon? He was still on her undecided list. She was not about to suggest that to Trace, though, or she'd take another teasing.

Trace and Darby met with Winslow and Cromwell in the manager's private office. The door was closed, and a curtain closed off a view of the reception area. This was a starkly different environment from the Mint office, Darby thought. She knew from her time here that each agent enjoyed a private office, although the junior agents might not be allotted more than closet space. This served to assure confidentiality for informants and protected operatives' paperwork from the prying eyes of office visitors or, God forbid, a rogue agent. Allan Pinkerton was not a fool who deceived himself that all his operatives put on halos the moment they pinned on their badges.

Jack Winslow told his visitors, "I've got four men to play pallbearers for the coffin tomorrow, and we'll put two or three operatives in the crowd for backup. You'll have all the available staff just in case something goes sour. Once the train pulls out, you're on your own, unless you want me to send some help. Pink said to give you whatever you want."

"No," Darby said. "We'll take it from there." Neither she nor Trace had mentioned Audra or Clay to anyone, agreeing that there was no reason to disclose the existence of their anonymous agents.

"Newt here will be one of the pallbearers so if there's any sudden change in plans, just let him know."

Trace said, "We will, but their job should be simple enough. When the gold crates are delivered, get two of the pallbearers in the boxcar and start transferring the gold bricks to the empty coffin. We'll be there to help speed up the transfer. When all the gold's in the coffin, seal it and slide the coffin to the open doorway and haul it away."

Newton Cromwell, sitting off to the side of the manager's desk, said, "We'll do our part."

Winslow said, "So, you think you can scare off this Blue Bandana gang with the Gatling Gun? I can see that. But the gold will be here in a Denver bank, so you're not protecting anything. I must be missing something here. I don't see the point of it. You're risking your necks to keep the damned outlaws from taking nothing."

Darby replied, "We hope to take down enough of them to put the outfit out of business. That's what Pink is paying us to do."

Darby could see Winslow wasn't buying her answer. She was fond of her former mentor, but she refused to lift the shroud of secrecy away from their mission.

"Well," Winslow said, "don't eat any bullets for lunch. We want to see you around here again sometime."

Chapter 14

TRACE AND DARBY returned to their Denver hotel room after their meeting at the Pinkerton office, comfortable that the mission was going as planned.

Winslow and Cromwell were to handle arrangements with the Mint office for delivery of the gold. Winslow had mentioned that Allan Pinkerton himself, through his connections to President Chester A. Arthur's Republican administration, had arranged for the order from the Philadelphia Mint to the Denver branch office. The question was whether the word had reached the Blue Bandana Gang by now. This was dependent on a spy or leaker at the Mint office as they suspected.

The next morning, Pinkerton agents would receive delivery of the bullion from the Mint's Denver office at the depot and load it onto the boxcar where Clay's coffins would be waiting, one containing the dismantled Gatling gun. The gold bars would be transferred from the packed chests to the empty coffin. When the delivery wagon from the Mint office was gone, the coffin bearing gold would be carried solemnly by agents to a waiting funeral carriage. It would then be delivered by the operatives to the vault of a local bank for temporary storage for several days prior to redelivery to the Mint office.

Darby sat down on the edge of the bed and began removing her high-button shoes. She kicked the shoes off and said, "I won't miss these things. It'll feel good to get back in riding gear again."

Trace removed his suitcoat and brushed it off before hanging it in the closet. "I guess we arrange to ship all the spare clothes back to Manhattan and hope they find their way home."

"You'd like the excuse to replace everything with something new anyway."

Trace said, "If everything works out the way we hope, I can afford a few new suits." He sat down and took off his boots, and then stood and dropped his britches and hung them in the closet with the coat.

"Don't count your chickens. We're a long way from those bonuses." She lay her own jacket and skirt over a chairback, wormed out of her silk blouse and slipped out of her chemise. She was naked now and pulled back the bedcovers and crawled beneath. "You make me feel slutty when you piddle like this."

"I thought we came up here to talk."

"We did. But we've got two hours before dinner this evening, and I assumed you might want to take advantage. There could be a long drought ahead."

"I hadn't even thought about it," he said, tugging off his undershorts.

She watched him as he approached the bed. "You lie. But your rascally friend never fails to tell the truth."

An hour later, Darby was sated. She was not a worldly woman in the way of carnal pleasures, but there was a lover before Trace, a boy who had left her pregnant at age sixteen. She had miscarried, been disowned by her Irish Catholic parents and remained chaste until the whirlwind romance with the man who shared her bed now blindsided her. But it seemed their lovemaking always took her places she had never visited before.

She had made an impulsive decision when she married this man, rejecting all common sense and caution that usually gave her pause. She was still learning about John Trace Crockett, and the more she learned, the more she liked him. Yes, "like," she thought. She knew she loved him, but "like" helped carry partners for the long haul.

He was so easy to be with, she had to feign a fuss sometimes just to liven things up a bit, and she suspected he did likewise. Disagreements, occasionally, yes. But not one had turned nasty. There was either compromise, or each took his or her own course. It was never necessary to declare a winner.

Trace lay next to her now, dozing and emitting the little purr she found both reassuring and endearing. She rolled on her side and nudged his back gently with her fist. He stirred and turned to face her.

"Not again," he groaned teasingly.

"We're here on business. We haven't been very professional. I don't think Allan would approve of this behavior in the middle of an assignment."

"That's why we started our own agency. We account for results, not time." Trace pulled the bedsheet up to his neck and tugged it over her shoulders as well. "But if we're going to talk business, we should remove the distractions."

She skootched up to the headboard and propped a pillow behind her back, but he remained on his side and placed his hand on her abdomen. "Trace," she scolded.

"Don't mind me."

"We need to discuss plans for tomorrow. Our waiting will be over then."

"I haven't been disturbed by the waiting. It's been like a honeymoon almost."

"An expensive honeymoon. You insisted on this pricey hotel for us. Then Audra's at the Fremont, which isn't cheap. Clay insisted on staying at the hotel near the station. I suppose that's where most colored lodgers stay, and train crews on layovers. Anyway, that's reasonable enough. But the lodging and meals all come out of the advance. There's a risk that's all we get out of the job."

"If that happens, Pink probably won't hire us again."

"That's why we need to get serious and talk about our plans." His hand moved to her small breast. Darby threw back the bedsheet, swung her legs over the side of the bed and leaped to her feet. She began searching out her undergarments.

She looked back at Trace, who remained in bed, watching her with an amused grin on his face as she dressed. "We'll tend to business better if we're not in bed," she said. "Besides, I'm hungry."

Trace rolled out of bed and commenced recovering his own garments, which had been laid out carefully and orderly. "I think everything's decided. We'll get to the station early and be sure the horses, tack and everybody's travel gear get loaded onto a livestock car and see that the coffins are on the boxcar. We wait for the gold and pall bearers. Clay and Audra won't recognize us if we cross paths. He'll be serving on the dining car, and Audra will be getting seated with passengers."

Darby said, "When everything's loaded, we climb aboard and close the door."

"Then I'll set up the Gatling gun. I hope you've got the lamp with your stuff."

"I do. Let's find a place to eat," she said.

"You're always wanting to find a place to eat, you and Audra. You and that tiny thing between you eat more than five starving lumberjacks. I don't see how either of you stays so skinny."

Chapter 15

AUDRA STUDIED THE depot platform from her window seat inside the passenger car. She had neither seen nor spoken to Darby and Trace for the past two days. She had encountered Clay Sibley when she was boarding the train, but they had intentionally not spoken. The Crockett detective group had separated prior to leaving the train upon arrival in Denver, deciding it would be best they not be identified as associates by any observers. She and Darby had lunched together after Darby and Trace met with detectives at the Pinkerton branch office the first day, and Darby had brought her up to date on progress of the plan.

Now she saw a short, fair-haired man in bib overalls, accompanied by a similarly attired colored man pulling a luggage cart bearing two crates in the direction of the box cars that trailed the passenger cars. That had to be the gold, she figured. The men, regardless of their dress, handled the cart rather clumsily, and were clean shaven and well-groomed in a way that signaled they were not run-of-the-mill manual laborers. They were no doubt Mint employees trying not to draw attention, and to the unpracticed eye, probably would not have.

The four suited men following the cart some distance behind were doubtless the Pinkerton National Detective Agency pallbearers. Their instructions were to wait until the gold crates were loaded and the deliverymen gone before stepping up to help transfer the gold to the empty coffin and haul the treasure to the awaiting hearse and accompany it to the bank. Darby and Trace should already be positioned in the boxcar to accept custody of the gold from the Mint.

She felt someone sit down beside her, and she turned to find a lanky man with leather vest and scuffed boots, and a gray Stetson pulled low on his forehead. His sun-bronzed face should have been shaved a few days back. She judged him to be mid-thirties. He smelled of sweat and cow shit, which she did not find pleasant, although Trace had told her several times that was money she smelled and that she should learn to appreciate it. She considered herself a ranch investor. Her financial interest did not require that she smell her investment.

"Howdy, ma'am. My name's Ted Colmes. Mind if I set myself down here?"

There were ample vacant seats in the car, but she did not want to attract attention by objecting. "No, that's quite all right."

She cast her eyes back toward the window and caught a glimpse of the Pinkerton agents walking slowly and almost synchronized across the platform with the coffin. Two shrill whistles, followed by the chugging of the engine, told her they would be moving out soon. The thought that this was the real beginning of her first mission as a Pinkerton operative launched butterflies in her stomach. She remembered again what Trace had told her once: it's never too late to become what you might have been. This was an important step away from her past. She truly believed that.

"Where you headed ma'am?" her seatmate asked, as the train pulled away.

Oh, no. She was not in the mood for conversation, and she needed to focus on the mission. "East."

"With due respect, ma'am, that don't tell me nothing."

"No, I suppose not."

"You ain't a talker, I guess."

Feeling guilty, she said, "I'm sorry. I don't mean to be rude. I'm not feeling well. I need to sleep, I think." She closed her eyes and pressed her head against the back of the seat.

Audra felt the seat shift when her would-be companion got up to seek out more congenial company.

Chapter 16

TRACE AND DARBY stood outside the boxcar, waiting for arrival of the two crates of gold bars. Upon their arrival, they had dropped bedrolls, their respective possible bags and a shared haversack in the boxcar, along with a kerosene lantern and hammer and crowbar. Trace had also brought a tubular-shaped canvas bag that carried their long guns, including a double-barreled shotgun, his Sharps rifle and Darby's Winchester. They both wore faded blue denims now and wide-brimmed hats. Trace's holstered Army Colt rested on his hip. Darby's sidearm was a .38 Baby Russian Smith & Wesson with a four-inch barrel, a treasure she had discovered at a Manhattan gunsmith's shop.

Trace looked at Darby, thinking his slender wife was even more striking in her riding garb. She stood not more than five and a half feet tall, but she cut an imposing figure on the station platform, and both men and women were casting furtive glances at her, some of the females revealing disapproval with their sour expressions. She would be blissfully unaware of the attention, of course. She thought of herself as rather plain. Some who did not see her through his eyes might not call her beautiful, but they would take notice of her. There was something in her bearing, the exquisitely carved features of her face and intelligent brown eyes that drew the attention of others. Fortunately, she was an expert at the art of disguise in a profession that occasionally demanded anonymity. Otherwise, she would rarely go unnoticed among a mass of people.

He heard the squeaking of the steel wheels of the luggage cart and turned his head toward the racket. Two men were pulling the load, and despite their workingman's attire, he tagged them as Mint employees instantly. There were likely a few others nearby, keeping an eye on the merchandise.

Shortly, the crates of bullion, weighing one hundred-fifty pounds each were loaded onto the floor of the boxcar. As soon as the Mint representatives departed, the Pinkerton pallbearers appeared. As promised, Newton Cromwell was with the party and clearly in charge. Cromwell and a hefty man, who probably weighed over two hundred-fifty pounds, Trace guessed, clambered into the boxcar.

"Do you want to keep an eye out, Darb?" Trace asked.

She nodded and remained outside with the other two Pinkertons while Trace followed Cromwell and his partner. With hammer and crowbar, they quickly dismantled the crates to reveal three hundred gold bars. The coffin containing the Gatling had been pushed up against the boxcar wall, and the empty coffin rested beside it. Trace removed the lid and placed it on top of the closed coffin.

"There should be ample space," Trace said, as they commenced stacking the gold bars in the coffin. "It'll be all four men will want to handle, but I assume you've got some help milling around the railroad yard, if you need it."

Cromwell said, "We should be okay. Big Jack here could carry the damn thing himself if need be."

Trace doubted that, but he did not question that the brawny man could carry more than his share of the load. As they transferred the bricks from crates to coffin, Big Jack worked quickly and efficiently, making up for Cromwell's slow pace. Trace figured the managing agent as a desk jockey who rarely lowered himself to physical labor. He was pleasant enough, but Trace wasn't sure he'd count on the man to have his back as an operative in the field.

But the agency needed paper shufflers, too, and Cromwell would not have risen to second in command at the busy Denver office without possessing some useful skills.

When the coffin was packed with bullion, Big Jack tacked on the lid. "I'll tell the boys to get ready," Cromwell said, stepping over to the wide cargo entrance. "We'll just slide it over, and they can take one end and pull it out, and we'll jump down and grab the other."

Just as Cromwell peered out, two gunshots cracked. Cromwell ducked and slipped a pistol from the shoulder holster hidden by his coat. Trace drew his Colt and came up behind him, noting that Darby, her Smith & Wesson raised, and the other Pinkertons seemed unharmed but were staring at the far end of the track. The few remaining passengers on the depot platform were running to board the train or headed for the station house for cover. "What is it, Darb?" Trace asked, dropping off the boxcar, followed by Cromwell.

"Somebody fired a few shots our way, but they didn't come close." She pointed toward a wooden tower below an elevated water tank. Trace caught a glimpse of movement behind a storage shed adjacent to the tower. Another wild shot. He raised his Colt and returned fire, squeezing off two quick shots. "Cover me," he yelled at Darby, who was following some ten paces behind him.

Trace charged the shed, watching for movement, and Darby trailed, her eyes searching for any accomplices. When Trace approached the little building, a horse and rider broke from behind the shed and raced away, following the track a short distance before cutting onto a dusty road that led away from the railroad yards. Trace did not even bother to fire a token shot. He turned back toward Darby.

"See anybody else?" he asked.

"Nobody. I don't know if he wanted to take us out or give us a scare."

"He was shooting a six-gun. An assassin doesn't use a six gun at that range."

They walked along the tracks adjacent to the boxcars and livestock cars. Trace noted that their horses seemed calm enough and was reassured by a whinny of recognition through the spaced boards from his buckskin stallion. When they reached their boxcar, the pallbearers were already sliding the coffin off the edge of the car floor, and Big Jack and Cromwell were easing their end down. Cromwell grunted when he accepted the weight of his corner of the coffin, and his knees started to buckle before he straightened up and tightened his gloved hand on the chain handle.

"Need some help?" Trace asked.

Cromwell smiled and shook his head. "Got it now. I'll be fine."

The train engine was signaling readiness and drowning out their voices. Trace turned to Darby just as the whistle blew. He waved at her to get on board. When they were in the car, he started to slide the door closed, then paused. "Darb, it will be pitch dark in here when I close the door. Want to light the lamp?" He reached in his front pocket, pulled out some lucifers and extended his hand. Darby snapped up the matches, and a few minutes later the lamplight rose like an early morning sunrise. Trace closed the door and slammed down the interior latch bar that was identical to the exterior mechanism. A person could be locked in or out, he thought. He flinched at the notion of not controlling the lock on both sides of the door.

"Well," he said, "I like the company but not the accommodations. I hope we don't have to make this trip more than once."

"At least this should tell us if the information source is in the Denver Mint office."

"But if it's not, we're back where we started. A helluva long way from finding Maddie Sanford or the gold stash—if it hasn't been scattered to the four winds by now."

The boxcar was rocking now, as the engine began to pull its cars away from the Denver station, and the clickety-clack of steel against steel began its rhythm. Trace thought it unlikely they would be hit by any robbers close to Denver, and he figured eastern Colorado or western Kansas most probable, miles between small railroad towns, routes north and south with vast spaces between settlements and farms. The Blue Bandanas had headed south after the last robbery and abduction of the girl, but since the trail was lost, that didn't mean a lot. The direction to that point could have been a diversion.

He pulled his pocket watch from his trouser pocket—he could not bear being without a timepiece—and checked the time: nine thirty-five. They shouldn't hit prime strike territory for several hours. He hoped the engineer had received the instructions from company headquarters to stop the moment he encountered a roadblock or recognized any track problems. After the last disastrous pileup, he supposed the instruction would be unnecessary. Better set up the gun. He could do the job in ten minutes, but it was better to be ready, leave nothing to chance.

Darby was sitting on the coffin, loading the shotgun, checking her Winchester. "Darb," Trace said, "let me get the Gatling parts out of the coffin, and you can have your seat back."

"I figured you wouldn't hold off long." She got up and moved her guns aside.

He picked up the crowbar and loosened the nails that held the lid down. Darby grabbed one end of the lid and he took the other, and they lifted it off and placed it on the floor.

Trace's stomach did a flip when he saw the contents. "Gold. I'll be damned. The dumb bastards took the wrong coffin. We've got the gold. Cromwell's crew made off with the Gatling."

Darby said, "You don't really think anybody was that dumb?"

"No. I think Cromwell's smarter than he looks. And now we don't know who to trust. We can't look to the Denver office for backup, even if we could reach them, that's for damn sure."

"And we've got the gold and no surprise for our Blue Bandana friends."

Chapter 17

MADDIE SANFORD AND her new friend, Minnie, lay on their bellies on the rock rim overlooking Copperhead Canyon. They were looking southeast where most of the cabins, lean-to sheds and outbuildings were located. They had chosen to exit the north side of the stream and canyons because Maddie knew generally what cities, including Denver, would lie to the north and west, although as far as she was concerned, those places might as well be located on the moon. The sun was creeping over the horizon, shooting blinding rays of light their way, but they still had a fair view of the canyon floor. There were no signs of activity yet, so their absence apparently so far had gone unnoticed. Cards and booze had likely granted the escapees time.

It had taken most of the night for them to make their way out of the canyon. The darkness had been their greatest enemy, luring them one way and then another that initially looked promising and then taking them to sheer walls not even a goat could climb. They had followed the small stream as planned and moved into the rocky channel as the canyon walls narrowed, water reaching waist-deep, as the fissure closed in.

They had emerged from the crack in the stone that led away from the canyon only to find they had entered another smaller canyon. They had debated following the stream to wherever it might lead but had agreed their trail would be too easy to track and that they would likely be rundown by their pursuers.

They had finally come across a deer trail used by wild creatures on journeys to fresh water, and after taking a dead end fork several times, backing up and trying again, they reached the summit and collapsed for a spell. Maddie suspected that Minnie's exhaustion was feigned for the purpose of giving her younger companion a rest because the woman moved with the grace of a panther over the stone outcroppings and ridges that erupted helter-skelter on the steep incline. She never sighed or stopped to catch a breath as Maddie did. Maddie thought if she were more noble, she should tell Minnie to go ahead without her. The outlaws would never catch her. Of course, where would she go? What would an uneducated Negro woman do when she found civilization? Maddie promised herself that if they escaped, she would find a way to help Minnie start a new and better life.

It was time for a decision. "I think we'd better move. It won't be long before they realize we took off," Maddie said. "I don't know why nothing happened when the guard came up missing, unless his relief didn't show up."

"It might could be. Cards and whiskey take over a man's head—more than woman sometime." She turned her head toward Maddie, and her eyes narrowed. "Y'all don't move," Minnie said, her voice barely above a whisper.

"What? Why?"

"Do what I says."

Minnie slowly raised herself to her knees and leaned back on her haunches. She eased her scissors-knife from her rope belt, and suddenly, she sprung, clearing Maddie's body and rolling beyond, rising to her knees, slicing at something writhing in her grip. A snake, and Minnie was clutching it tightly behind its head as she held it fast against the stone canyon rim and sawed with the crude blade. Soon the reptile's head rolled away, and she held the writhing, bleeding body and tail in her hand. "Big sumbitch," she said, "for copperhead." She gave a flick of her wrist and the creature dropped over the canyon's rim.

Maddie got up and moved away from the edge of the canyon rim. "My God, Minnie, you saved my life." Maddie found herself trembling uncontrollably. The incident had all happened so fast, her fear had not struck till it was over.

Minnie put a consoling arm around Maddie's shoulders. "Y'all be okay. Copperheads be all over place. Why the name, I s'pose. No rattle, like some. Smoke get bite. Got sick, but y'all see, didn't die. Killed snake and make me cook it up for suppertime. Good luck, he say."

"But you just grabbed the thing and killed it."

"Ain't nothing, Sweets. Got moccasins all over where I come from. Kill devils all time."

Maddie was collecting herself now. "We need to get moving."

"Y'all go. I come along."

Minnie had made it clear from the beginning that she had no idea where they were in relation to a possible destination, or what that destination might be. Maddie was only slightly ahead of her friend on that score. She knew if they walked far enough, they would eventually reach a railroad track which could be followed westward to some small town along the line and eventually to Denver. On foot, she supposed, the track would be many days distant, or, perhaps, weeks. They had food for a few days at best. Their water supply would not hold out that long, and her father had warned her often about the dangers of drinking non-boiled water, unless water flowed from an uncontaminated source, such as a spring from a stone wall.

"Minnie," Maddie said, "I've never asked. Besides the food and some water, what do you have in your bag?"

Minnie opened the bag. "Y'all look."

Maddie knelt and rummaged through the bag. Rope, quite a lot of it. The wrapped food. Two canteens. Ammunition salvaged from the dead guard. "Do you have lucifers?"

"Yes, Sweets. In tin box."

She continued the inventory. A small metal pot. A bundle of rags. Bottle of whiskey. She wasn't sure about the rags and whiskey, but she supposed the woman had her reasons. The pot and lucifers could be handy for boiling water for drinking or cooking. Maddie stood up and picked up her rolled buffalo robe.

She started walking north, wincing as sharp stones stabbed the bottoms of her feet through the moccasins Minnie had furnished. Better than nothing, she guessed.

After her hours of confinement, she had initially welcomed the sunshine and open spaces, but several hours later, she was having second thoughts. The torrid sun was taking a toll, and shade was hard to come by here. She had never visited a desert, but this barren land reminded her of what such a place might be like. She had seen pictures of the occasional cholla cactus that popped up in otherwise plant-starved terrain here. Fine red dirt intermingled with the shale and rock fragments to form their pathway. Small buttes and ragged stone formations rose from the ground about them, and gullies and arroyos crisscrossed the landscape. It was mostly a desolate place, but several times she had seen small carpets of short grass prairie not unlike the kind that cloaked the vast valley of the Sanford family's Colorado ranges. Deer and goats and tough, resilient breeds of cattle could graze and survive in this land.

They had stopped to rest several times when they came upon a lonely cottonwood and cluster of scraggly junipers, the latter smelling of bobcat or cougar piss, the distinctive odor which she had come to know during her happy ranch days. She knew the rest breaks continued for her benefit because Minnie seemed unfazed by the trek to nowhere. Maddie paused a moment, feeling faint and realizing her walking had turned to staggering.

They had not slept last night, and she was fading now. She must find a place to nap. Even a half hour would help. Her eyes searched the horizon and sighted a stand of cottonwoods, one towering and ancient. There were smaller unidentifiable trees and brush surrounding the cottonwoods, a miniature forest, she thought. And a good chance for water.

She turned to speak to Minnie, but her friend had disappeared again. She had departed earlier for an hour, explaining she was back-tracking to see if the search by their former captors had started, or if someone had picked up their trail. Maddie did not care anymore. She just wanted to lie down. She opened the canteen Minnie had handed her earlier, tipped it to her lips and savored the remaining few drops, and, at the same time, chided herself for not rationing the water more prudently.

Eyes focusing on the cottonwood grove, Maddie trudged ahead, weaving and stumbling, but her mind fixed on the goal. When she got there, she was delighted to find a carpet of grass beneath the overhanging branches of the trees, which included a few sturdy oaks, vegetation she had not yet seen in this godforsaken country. And a clear stream gurgled nearby, calling her to bathe in its waters and to drink its inviting contents. She resisted and dropped to the ground, softened by the thick grass.

She untied the buffalo robe and spread it out, crawled on top, curled up, and closed her eyes.

When Maddie awakened almost two hours later, she found Minnie sleeping beside her on the robe. She sat up and saw the dying fire coals with the pot sitting off to one side. Minnie had obviously boiled some drinking water. Maddie got up and went over to the pot and picked it up. It was warm to the touch, so the water should be drinkable.

Minnie's voice came from behind her. "I done drunk mine, Sweets. Drink what y'all wants, then fill y'alls jug. I put two them ribs and a biscuit just inside my bag. Better y'all eat and we gets going 'cause Miss Trouble on her way."

Maddie took the kettle in both hands and was soon slurping water, enjoying the sensation of the fluid dribbling down her cheeks and neck. When she pulled the container away from her lips, she said, "I'd love to take a bath. What do you mean by 'trouble'?"

"Mens is moving in the canyon. They come on fast like old swamp gators when they gets our scent. And Bull, he gets it. I promise that. Bath later, maybe."

"Can we go upstream along the bank?"

"Till we finds a hole-up place. Then we sleep more and go when dark comes."

Chapter 18

B Y THEIR THIRD day on the run, the food supply had disappeared and not even a biscuit crumb was available for breakfast. They had stopped their trek several hours after midnight because they had found a man-made cave carved out in a sandstone mesa wall. Why anyone would build a cave in this isolated place, Maddie could not imagine. By the near-suffocating odor and tufts of hair scattered about the shallow cave, it was obvious that the hideout had most recently been occupied by a black bear.

Minnie had evidently awakened earlier and departed for one of her increasingly frequent scouts. She was speaking less with each return. Maddie did not take that as a positive sign and decided she would press her friend today.

She and Minnie had both bathed in the stream before heading for the cave and the warm buffalo robe. The robe's repulsive smell had been overcome by bear stench, but it felt cozy and comforting against naked flesh. She had slipped into shirt, britches and moccasins upon rising and sat now with legs dangling over the ledge in front of the cave, less than five feet above the ground. An orange glow radiating fingers of light was just reaching above the eastern horizon, but sunlight was an hour away, Maddie figured.

Soon she caught a glimpse of movement to the south. It was Minnie, of course, her long rhythmic strides carrying a ghostly shadow through the pre-dawn duskiness. When she arrived, she trotted up to Maddie, and her grim face was not encouraging.

"There be three mens. Smoke, Bull and Moon. All walk."

Moon, the man who had raped and beaten her. Instinctively, she reached for her Winchester. "How far back?" Maddie asked.

Minnie looked puzzled and appeared to be pondering the question. "Two hour, little more. Y'all get ready to run."

Maddie scooted back into the cave and commenced rolling up the robe, while Minnie retrieved her bag of assorted items. Soon they had their scant possessions gathered.

Maddie asked, "Shall we find a place to ambush them?"

"Bull know. Can't fool him. Y'all and me splits now. Y'all go that way." She pointed north. "I run that way," she said, signaling she would head west.

"But how will we find each other?"

"Can't see it now, but when sun comes up, y'all see mountains. Seen them yesterday. Go there. Hide and I find y'all."

Maddie found herself shaking with fright. This woman had become more than kin in their brief time together. The thought of separation was unbearable. "We should stay together," she protested.

Minnie shook her head vigorously. "No. No chance that way. Go now. Follow stream but leave soon. Go to mountains, Sweets." She handed her bag to Maddie. "Y'all take this, too."

"But why, if we're going to meet up? I don't understand."

"Y'all stay on rock as much y'all can. Harder track y'all."

"But you said Bull can track anything."

"Bull be dead. Now go, Sweets."

Maddie stepped forward and took the skinny, dark woman in her arms and held her like a lifeline. "Be careful, Min. Don't do anything foolish. You're the best friend I ever had. I love you. I want to see you again." She stepped back, tears streaming down her cheeks.

Minnie's eyes were wide and teary like she could not believe the words she had heard. "Loves y'all, too, Sweets. Go."

Reluctantly, Maddie picked up her rifle, robe and bag and turned away. She headed north along the stream for a spell before deciding to walk in the streambed for a time, despite moving against the current. She hoped it might cause her pursuers to lose her trail or at least slow their progress. She looked back over her shoulder and saw Minnie still standing where she had left her. She waved, and her friend waved back.

Later, knowing that the water was slowing her pace too much, she stepped out of the stream, hoping she had at least delayed any followers. The sun had blossomed to full light now, and she could see the black, hazy outline of the mountains Minnie had spoken of, not as far reaching as her beloved Rockies and no apparent sky-reaching peaks, but mountains, nonetheless. She angled north-westerly through rock formations and arroyos, which at first seemed a maze. But the mountains were her compass, leading to her intended destination.

Then she heard the popping and cracking, like an Independence Day celebration, to the south. Oh, God. Minnie. And it struck her. Minnie had made herself a decoy. She had been waiting for the pursuers to appear so she could lead them away from Maddie. How could she have been so blind? The gunfire quieted for several minutes, and then it recommenced just briefly before silence settled over the savage land.

She identified a stone formation that erupted from the earth like a giant, half-bell and took her robe and bag and set them down at the base. She plucked a handful of cartridges from Minnie's bag and stuffed them in the front pocket of her britches. She snatched the canteen by the little shoulder rope Minnie had fashioned, and with her rifle cradled in her arm, headed in the direction of the gunfire. At best, she hoped to intercept her friend, or, perhaps, tend to her wounds. At worst, she would see Minnie properly buried so coyotes and other predators would not desecrate her remains.

She had a sense of foreboding. Minnie would have told her that her quest was nonsense, but she had to know. She did not know how long she had walked, an hour, maybe two. She likely never would have found the place had not the vultures, those circling, black harbingers of death, summoned her.

Maddie ran toward the gliding, swooping birds of prey. Fifteen minutes later, she slowed and moved more stealthily among the rocks. She froze when she came upon the scene. Sprawled out on the ground was the Indian called Bull, the front of his shirt smeared with blood, browning quickly in the hot sun. Off to one side some ten paces distant, the Negro, Smoke, sat with his back against a huge boulder, blood pumping from a shoulder wound. His knee appeared to have been injured also. He seemed to be dazed, unaware of her presence, but a pistol was clutched in his hand.

But where was Min? She stepped forward, her Winchester pointed at Smoke's chest. "Let go of your gun, mister."

He looked up at her with glazed-over eyes. "Help me." His voice was weak and raspy.

"Drop your damn gun."

He looked down at his hand, slowly opened his fingers and released the weapon, watching it fall in the dirt. Rifle still pointed at the man's chest, Maddie walked over to him and kicked the gun away.

"Where's Minnie?"

"The whore bitch? Kilt her dead. Me and Moon. After she killed Bull. We caught up to her. Didn't have no gun in her holster. She walks up to Bull, arms out like she was glad to see him. Sudden-like, there's a gun in her hand, pokes the barrel in his chest and fires twice. Must've pulled it out of her ass. Bull falls and next thing, crazy bitch turns it on me. Hit my shoulder, but I got a couple slugs in her. She shot my knee bone when she was going down."

"Where is she? Damn it."

"Help me."

"Tell me where she is. Then I'll help you."

"Over there. That gully. Moon tossed her there after he put a couple shots in her head. She was down, and Moon stripped her naked. Was gonna have some of her before she died. She weren't as close to dead as we thought. He dropped his britches and got down to take her, and she swings a knife at his balls. Missed but come close and stabbed inside his thigh. Bled some but not hurt bad. Anyhow, that done it, he finished her for good. Damned wildcat that bitch was."

"Where's Moon?" Maddie asked.

"Hunting for you, I suppose. Figures he's a dead man if he don't take you back. You took off on our watch, and Bax don't like the Comanch kid nohow. Think he looks to have some fun when he catches you . . . if he ain't too crippled."

"But he left without you."

"Couldn't walk. Said he he'd send somebody back for me. Yeah. When hell freezes over. Ain't gonna happen. Be dead by then anyhow." He started to cry.

Maddie picked up the pistol and threw it as far as she could, and then she walked slowly toward the gully, dreading what she was going to find there.

"Hey, girl," Smoke called. "You said you was gonna help me."

"Shut up," she yelled back. When she reached the gully, she looked down into the three-foot crevice and saw the naked, crumpled body, her shredded shirt and skirt lying at her feet. She put down her rifle and slid into the gully, straightening out the body, gently pressing the eyelids shut. She sat down and cradled Minnie's head in her lap, tracing her fingers about the wounds in the mulatto woman's neck and head, surprised at the lack of blood about the bullet entries. Minnie's stomach and chest were caked with blood and dirt, though, and she wondered how her friend had somehow got off the shots that hit Smoke, let alone struck out at Moon with the homemade knife.

She sobbed quietly for some minutes in the silence of the vast wasteland while shadows of soaring vultures swept back and forth over her face. Finally, she summoned up the resolve to do what she must do. When she scrambled out of the arroyo, she picked up her rifle and walked back to Smoke, who was still conscious and seemed more alert than when she had found him.

"Help me," he said. "Patch my shoulder and knee. I know I can walk. You just rustle up a branch or something for a crutch or cane. You get me back to the canyon, and I won't let nobody hurt you, I promise."

She lifted the Winchester and aimed.

"What you doing, gal? You can't..."

Smoke's words were cut off when she squeezed the trigger and the rifle cracked. She had never heard a rifle thunder like that. She wondered why not. A second shot was unnecessary. The first struck between the eyes. She had put him down, and it wasn't much different than the time she had watched her father end the misery of a gelding that had broken its leg. Except the gelding had been hers and she had grieved.

Today she had killed her first man and found herself untroubled by it. She had heard her late lover, Wally, say once that some folks just needed killing, but she could not shrug it off that easily. Wally had fancied himself a gunfighter, and that did not seem so glamorous as it once did. Killing for fame or adulation, or even notoriety. She did not want to be like that. She would think on it if she lived long enough. Maybe she would feel something again, too, someday.

She had work to take care of now. She would need to keep an eye out in case her gunshot brought Moon back this way. She thought it unlikely, though. A single shot. Moon would probably figure Smoke had done himself in or shot at a coyote or something. Still, she didn't like not knowing where Moon was at.

It was a bit of a struggle, but she worked Smoke's shirt off his corpse. Bull's shirt was a greater challenge, because his body was starting to stiffen, and it required some effort to maneuver his arms. The shirts were huge, for the wearers had been near giants. She hated that the garments were bloodied, but this was the best she could do. She wrapped the shirts about Minnie's body. She shuddered at the notion of pushing dirt on top of her friend's naked flesh, though her head told her it didn't matter. The worms and insects would clean her bones anyway.

The small rocks and dirt on the sides of the gully caved in easily over Minnie's body. After she had pushed in as much of the mix as she could to cover the body, Maddie carried and rolled stones to layer the top and discourage digging by animals. She found an unusual black stone with a strange fissured and pocked surface to mark the grave. She observed a near triangle of cholla plants less than five feet from the burial place. They would help identify the spot if they did not disappear before her return. She hoped they would thrive and keep Minnie company.

When she finished, she stood above the gravesite and examined the results of her labor. "If I live to do it, Minnie, I'll come back to visit from time to time. I promise. And you will always be with me, in my heart." She bowed her head. "God, I never even knew Minnie's last name, if she had one. She lived her life the best she could with the cards that were dealt her, and she became my angel. I haven't been around much lately and won't ask anything for me, but if you've got a heaven up there, and you really are a just God, you've got to let her in. That's all I'm praying for right now. Amen."

She turned away and gave a few quick glances at the corpses of the two outlaws and decided she would get on her way and let the buzzards and their friends start dinner. She studied the rock formations and other landmarks briefly, filing them in her memory so she could find the place again someday. She would need to ration her water, but the sun would be dying out for the day well before she got back to the buffalo robe and Minnie's bag. And she had spotted a spring along the way. If worse came to worse, she'd fill the canteen with non-boiled water. Sometimes, as her dad often said, you've got to pick your poison, take your chances.

As she headed back into the maze laid out by this formidable land, it occurred to her she was no longer afraid. Not of danger that might lie ahead. Not even of death. She was no longer the Maddie Sanford of several weeks ago. And she had an angel sitting on her shoulder.

Chapter 19

BAXTER CORKER DID not like the table-like prairies of this part of western Kansas. The Blue Bandana crew was staging the robbery on the Kansas side of the Kansas-Colorado line. The escape route would be mostly south to No Man's Land and then west to the Copperhead Canyon hideout, but the first half of the journey would take a day across wide-open lands, much of it now starting to be broken up into farmland occupied by a farmhouse on every quarter section. They would not pass unnoticed, and there were few places to hole up and hide or make a stand with the law on their tails.

Most small towns along the way had telegraph offices now, and word would no doubt get out to the law well before they made the canyon. For his part, he would like to see the gang go back to bank jobs. Smaller takings, maybe, but less preparation. Hit quick and run.

This should be a nice haul, and it seemed unlikely that the engineer would try to break through the barrier after the wreckage and carnage that resulted in the big haul a few weeks back. They had gotten away with gold that day, but killing the Pinkerton guards, a half dozen passengers and the engineer and fireman had placed the Blue Bandanas on every wanted poster with bounties high enough to bring out the fortune hunters. He hoped to bring off this job with no killings, at least none that were not essential.

He sat on his mount in a ravine split by a creek some distance back from the small trestle over which the train would ordinarily pass. They had removed a few sections of track from the trestle and pushed them into the creek and stacked ties on the track over a hundred feet distant from the creek crossing. His idea was to give the engineer ample time to see the obstruction and bring the train to a stop even if it struck the barrier.

Stick Holdrege edged his black gelding up next to Corker. "We got a dozen men, Bax. I'm thinking we could spare three for a collection right off, while the rest of us take care of the gold car."

Corker sighed. "I guess it won't hurt none. And we don't want to hang around this place. Get the gold packed on the two mules, and we get the hell out. Don't want to be waiting for a collection after. How about Jim-Bob, Pete Morales and that fat guy from the other crew?"

"They call the fat guy 'Pork.' Yeah, he's been around some, not a friendly guy, but he ain't likely to go shooting for the fun of it. Not like that crazy Moon."

"Okay, tell the guys to take care of it, and Pete's in charge."

The distant train whistle caught Corker's attention. He would know soon if the engineer was going to cooperate and make things easy.

Chapter 20

AUDRA WAS SITTING at a table in the dining car when the train slowed and finally stopped. She had just finished off a nice roast beef and cheese sandwich and was waiting for Clay to return with a slice of apple pie. He looked quite handsome in his white coat and black bow tie, she thought, as he walked toward her. On the other hand, she had never seen him when he appeared less than dashing.

He placed the plate on the table. "I saw riders out there wearing the blue bandanas. We can look for company soon."

"Are you armed?"

He pulled back his jacket slightly to reveal his shoulder holster that carried a pistol. "Enough for now. My .45 Schofield short barrel. Got my long barrel and a Henry rifle with the gear we stashed with the horses."

She patted her thigh. "Derringer holstered here. My .44 Smith & Wesson's in my bag." She stood up. "Hate to pass up the pie, but I'd better get back to my seat."

"I'll stick around till I see what plays out here. Then I'll get back to the horses. We can't let them get turned out."

"Trace wants a live prisoner," she reminded him.

"If they come aboard, we'll try to fix him up with one."

Audra returned to her seat. There were two passenger cars in addition to the new Pullman dining car positioned between the two. One car trailed the engine and fuel car, and Audra was seated in the car furthest from the engine. The "cattle car" utilized for horses this trip was next, and she had chosen her seat, so she could step out and keep her eye on the horses from time to time. Three freight cars followed the horses, the last, nearest the caboose, carrying the Gatling gun and Pinkerton guards.

"What the hell's going on," yelled the cowboy from his seat several rows ahead of her. She hoped his mouth would not prove fatal.

The car was slightly more than half full, perhaps fifteen passengers, the majority women and children. This worried her some because wild gunfire did not discriminate between age and gender. Outside of the cowboy, the four other men on the car were attired in business suits, signaling that they were from the world of commerce or professionals. None carried guns openly displayed. There was a single conductor to tend to the passengers in both cars, but he was not in her car just now.

Momentarily, a man with a blue kerchief pulled over his face and a pistol clutched in his right hand opened the door facing Audra, who sat near the opposite end of the car. "Okay, folks," the muffled voice behind the bandana said. "Take your guns, those who got them, and toss them in the aisle. Do what I say, and nobody gets hurt."

There was an anxious clamor of voices among the women, who were gathering their children like mother hens with chicks. The men were silent. One of the businessmen tossed a small pistol in the aisle. She noticed the cowboy had not disarmed. She, of course, had no intention of surrendering her weapons and figured she would not be suspected of carrying one, let alone two.

"Now," the gunman said, "we're going to take up a collection." He tugged a big flour sack from his back pocket and spread it open. "When I walk down this aisle, I'm going to pick up your money and your jewels. That includes watches, necklaces and the like. Ladies, if you can't work a ring off your finger, just hold up the finger." He caressed the handle of a skinning knife sheathed on his hip. "I'll take the finger, if I need to." There was a sob from a young woman a few seats ahead and across the aisle from Audra, who clutched two small children in her arms.

"Now, my friend's going to be coming from the back and he'll start the collection from that end. You just scoot down your seat towards the window and start emptying your wallets and pocketbooks on the end of the seats near the aisle. Put the rings and watches and necklaces there, too. Try holding out on us, and you're going to pay dear. We ain't looking to kill, so long as you help us out, but we won't lose no sleep if you force our hand that way. Just do what I'm telling you."

Audra tossed a look over her shoulder and caught a glimpse of a big man with a pendulous belly and porcine eyes to match. He was bent over, gun in one hand, sack in the other, clumsily trying to scrape a few watches, a ring and cash off the seat into the bag. Empty wallets had been laid there for his inspection. "You're holding out," he told the middle-aged man nearest the window and pointed the pistol at him.

"I forgot," the man said lamely and reached in his coat pocket and pulled out a roll of bills, handing it to his seat-mate, who dropped it on the edge of the seat. The outlaw squeezed the pistol trigger and the roar echoed through the passenger car. Blood and brain tissue splattered on the window next to the holdout, and the man slumped over. His companion, whose shirt and face were sprinkled with scarlet, leaned toward the dead man. "Frank . . . Frank," he choked. He turned to the shooter, his eyes tearful and face enraged. "You've killed my brother, you son-of-a-bitch."

Audra reached into her bag, and her fingers closed on the grip of her Schofield, fearing she must act before the outlaw shot the other man. Before she could slip the gun out, however, the gunman slammed the pistol barrel against the man's temple, flattening him back in the seat. The outlaw gathered the rest of his loot and took a few steps toward Audra. If the secreted gun did not get her killed, she figured the Pinkerton badge in her bag would.

The Blue Bandana at the front yelled, "That didn't have to happen. He didn't listen. Don't make this happen again." The speaker was shaken by developments. She could tell by the quiver in his voice. Another gun dropped in the aisle from one of the men up front. Then the cowboy tossed his out. The contributions from the passengers were coming in quickly now. She looked up, and saw the big man towering over her.

"Make it fast, lady," he growled.

She tipped her bag, her hand still clutching the Smith & Wesson, and spilled the contents on the end of the bench seat. Audra's hand still buried in the empty bag, her finger moved to the trigger and she squeezed. The explosion and kick stunned her for an instant before she squeezed the trigger again. The outlaw grunted and dropped his weapon, and it clattered to the floor. He clutched his chest, his eyes wide with obvious disbelief, and then his knees buckled, and he collapsed.

She pulled her gun from the bag and swung to face the other outlaw. But he was gone, and Clay stood in his place, pistol in his hand.

"Got him down," he told her. "He's a live one. Hold him. Got to go." He turned and raced back toward the dining car.

Still holding her pistol, Audra snatched up her Pinkerton badge and leaped from her seat, hurrying down the aisle and waving the badge, hollering "Pinkerton agents. Pinkerton agents."

She knelt by the prostrate form stretched out on the aisle floor and yanked the bandana off his face. Not more than a kid, fair-haired, pathetic patch of chin whiskers and sparse moustache. The side of his head was bleeding and swollen where Clay's pistol butt had struck. He was not likely to be waking anytime soon, but she thought he would eventually come around.

She stood up and looked around. The car was consumed by silence, and all eyes were on her. Traces of a smile were on the cowboy's lips, and he was nodding approvingly. She spoke to him, "Sir, would you collect the bags and take charge of returning the money and personal items to these folks?"

"I'd be pleased, ma'am. And I, for one, thank you and your friend for saving our skins and our valuables today."

His words broke the spell. Others started expressing their appreciation and the chatter of excited voices took over. Audra returned to her seat, recovered her own bag, still functional despite two bullet holes, and put her own belongings back, holding back a leather pouch in which she had packed two sets of handcuffs. She tugged out one pair and went back to the outlaw and cuffed his hands behind his back. He was stirring some now but would not be causing any trouble.

She hated to impose again on the cowboy after the way she had brushed him off earlier, but he seemed most unfazed about all the chaos, and he had a sidearm holstered to his hip. "Sir, could I ask you to keep an eye on this man while I check on my partner?"

"I'd do that if you'll call me 'Ted.' Don't know 'sir.'"

"Done. I'm Audra, and I apologize for being unfriendly earlier."

"That's all right. I understand now."

She heard two gunshots in the direction of the front passenger car and wheeled, snatched up her gun and headed that way.

Chapter 21

C LAY WALKED SOFTLY through the vacant dining car and stepped into the vestibule that connected the room to the front passenger car. He
pressed his back to the sidewall when he caught sight of
the gun-toting man moving up the aisle with the gunny
sack in his hand. He was encouraged that calm seemed to
be prevailing in the car. There were no more than a doz-
en passengers, but Clay did not want to risk a single life
needlessly. He decided to let the man finish the collection
and hope he planned to exit into the dining car and meet
up with his friends.

He guessed the stocky man to be Mexican, but who
knew? And it didn't matter. All that counted was the
man's skill with a gun. Clay moved his head just enough
to gauge the man's progress and saw that the outlaw had
reached the last passenger. His grip tightened on the

Schofield when he saw the outlaw moving away from the last victim and in the direction of the dining car. He waited, but not having more than a half foot of cover, he anticipated being spotted soon.

Clay heard the door of the passenger car squeak open and the man's accented words, "What the hell?"

Clay stepped out, gun poised to fire, but the outlaw got off a shot first, and Clay felt the burning in his neck, just beneath his jaw, before he fired his own weapon and drove a slug into his adversary's chest. The man staggered a few steps backward before dropping both gun and bulging sack and tumbling back into the passenger car.

"Clay? Are you okay?" It was Audra's voice from the dining car.

He touched his fingers to his stinging neck, and feeling the sticky wetness there, pulled back blood-coated digits. "Better than he is," Clay said, pointing to the legs protruding from the passenger car door.

Audra moved toward him. "Your neck. You've been hit. Get in here and sit down." She grabbed his arm and led him to the dining room, where he dropped into a chair at one of the tables.

"Get that white coat off," Audra ordered. "Then lay your head on the table."

Clay obeyed, pulling off the coat, rolling it up and placing it on the tabletop, where he rested his head. Audra snatched up a linen napkin, and Clay could feel her wiping away the blood from the wound.

"Dug a groove along the side of your neck. Less than three inches long. Bled out nice and cleaned the wound. For now, I just want to staunch the bleeding. I'm going to take another napkin and fold it, then you press it tight until I find something to anchor it with."

"Yes, ma'am. You've patched wounds before?"

"More than a few. Let's just say I haven't lived a sheltered life."

Audra disappeared for a moment into the kitchen area and soon returned with a carving knife. She commenced slicing on the tablecloth and tore away long strips, one of which she quickly slapped over the napkin packing and cinched around Clay's neck. "I'll save the other for redressing," she said. "Lift your head."

He raised his head and stretched his neck. "Thanks," he said. "That'll do fine." Before he could embellish the compliment, gunfire from outside grabbed his attention.

Audra said, "It's coming from the rear of the train. But it's not a Gatling gun, is it?"

"No. It's not a Gatling gun. I'd better check it out. If only I had my Henry rifle."

"The outlaws." She walked to one side of the car and peered outside, then wheeled and went to the other side and looked through a window. "Two horses hitched to the handrails outside the front car. One must have tied his someplace else. But there are rifles in saddle scabbards on both. I'm sure they're loaded. Probably extra cartridges in the saddle bags. I'm going with you, of course."

"But we got a prisoner to look after."

"You go ahead. I've got a new cowboy friend helping out. I'll go explain to him. Damn. My boots and britches are with the gear we put in the cattle car. Sure would like to trade these skirts off right now."

Chapter 22

"ANY IDEAS, DARB?" Trace asked, as they waited inside the boxcar for guests to arrive. Trace had suggested they surrender the gold without a fight. He said the gang leader would be reluctant to add up more deaths. They would track them later.

She had been disappointed in his willingness to give up the bullion. That was not the Trace she had come to know. It had finally dawned on her that she was responsible for his reluctance to fight. He was thinking about the killings of the other Pinkerton resistors.

"Yes," she said. "We don't surrender. Trace, if we let the gold get away, we can forget about any future Pinkerton work. And if we turn over the gold, they're not going to leave our horses in the cattle car so we can chase after them. They'll be taking the mounts along. If that happens, we've let this gold get away and can't track the gang, so we've lost any chance of recovering the other bullion and the girl. Even if Cromwell leads us to the head of the snake, that won't be enough to satisfy Pink."

"I know that. I just feel responsible for the Gatling getting away and don't want you to pay the price for it."

"Are we partners or not?"

"Of course, we're partners."

"Well, this partner votes to keep the gold."

Trace shrugged, "I'm with you. I was having to swallow hard on this one. And I've been thinking about it. We were going to surprise them with the Gatling. I was just going to have you slide the door open some and I'd start firing. If we're going to have any chance at all, we've still got to deliver a surprise."

"Tell me what you want me to do."

Fifteen minutes later, they stood in the pitch blackness of the freight car, the bullion-filled coffin resting next to the door. Someone hammered on the door with a hard object, probably a rock, Darby thought.

"Who is it?" Trace hollered.

"Your friendly neighbor dropping by for a visit. Don't give me that shit. You know who the hell we are."

"What do you want?"

"Ain't playing more games. Now open up, damn it, or we blow you out with a few sticks of dynamite."

"I suppose you want the gold."

"Say, you're a smart boy. Must've had some schooling."

Trace said, "We turn over the gold, and you let us go?"

"All we want is the gold. We ain't got cause to kill nobody. Just stay out of the way, and nobody gets hurt."

"We're not coming out, but we've got a coffin full of gold. We'll slide it up next to the door. I'll open the door long enough for you to take it, and then I close back up."

"Coffin?"

"The gold's stacked in a coffin."

"If you're lying about that, you're a dead man."

"Fair enough."

"I'm going to slide the door open."

"Ready?" Trace whispered to Darby.

"Open the door."

He slid the door open, exposing the coffin. Three men were there to grab it, and another was dismounting to assist. Darby could make out several mounted men further back with rifles cradled in their arms. Two men reached out to pull the coffin from the boxcar just as Darby squeezed the shotgun trigger. The weapon kicked and jolted her shoulder, but the resulting explosion rammed buckshot into at least two and, possibly, a third man, erupting a shower of blood.

Trace stepped out briefly and got off a few wild shots with his Colt before dodging back. Then, after Darby launched the second shotgun blast, he slid the door closed, gathered up his Sharps and prepared for whatever was to come next. Darby was reloading her shotgun when he stepped over beside her.

"How many went down? I don't know if I hit anybody," Trace said. "I know two won't be riding out of here. They dropped like stones. Another was crawling away."

"I think my second round did damage, but the outlaws weren't close in. They didn't go down—at least not right away."

"Well, we're out of surprises now, and I doubt if they're going to call it quits that easy. Of course, we don't have a count. We'd better get away from the door. It wouldn't be that hard for somebody to get it open and stay clear of our gunfire. The dynamite talk worries me some."

"The reports of the last robbery said they tried that then, but it apparently backfired. They might not be so quick to make that move."

They separated and took up positions on each side of the doorway, leaving the coffin between them, figuring it would slow entry by any attacker and furnish some cover if they dropped behind it. Darby figured the smallest edge could make the difference between life and death.

After what seemed an interminable silence, Darby heard excited voices outside, signaling preparation for a serious onslaught. She caressed the grip of the S & W Russian holstered on her hip but opted again for the double-barreled shotgun. Besides reducing the need for fancy shooting, the firearm was an intimidating force. Her right shoulder would be immobile and covered with a massive bruise tomorrow, though. She hoped she lived to feel the pain.

Suddenly, the door was being slid back, and she got a glimpse of a man moving with it. She raised the shotgun, hesitating to waste a shot at a barely visible target. From his position, Trace would have no view whatsoever. Then, several rifle cracks sounded, and the man stumbled and went down before finishing his task. There was more gunfire outside, but it was not directed at the occupants of the boxcar. She peered out and saw that the outlaws' attention was focused up the track in the direction of the passenger cars. Another Blue Bandana attacker was crumpled on the ground some ten paces from the boxcar. Several mounted riders were returning fire, while two others scrambled for their horses.

Darby and Trace had been all but forgotten by the outlaws. Trace stepped out, planted one foot on the coffin and got off a shot with the powerful Sharps, catapulting a rider from his saddle. The target's body landed on the hard earth, raising dust puffs as it settled motionless there. The Blue Bandanas that were still mounted, turned and raced their horses away. Darby counted four riders, and one leaned forward in the saddle like he might be wounded.

"The cavalry showed up in the nick of time," Trace said.

They climbed over the coffin that still obstructed the entrance and dropped off the boxcar. Darby looked up the tracks and saw Audra crawling out from under the cattle car with her Winchester in hand.

"Everybody okay?" Darby started at the sound of the voice above her, and her gaze shifted to the boxcar's top, where Clay stood surveying the scene, rifle slung over his shoulder.

"All okay for Trace and me. I think you'll need to make five more coffins, though."

"Plus two," Clay said. "Audra and I have two laid out up front." He turned and headed toward the end of the boxcar. "I'm coming down." He disappeared between two boxcars, and, when he was on the ground, joined Darby, falling in just a few paces behind Audra.

Trace, who had been checking the scattered bodies for any signs of life, came up behind Darby and wrapped an arm about her shoulders. "Thanks, Clay and Audra. If you hadn't shown up, one way or the other, they'd likely have run us out."

Clay said, "We thought there might be trouble. I never heard the Gatling gun. Jam on you?"

"Nope. We got the gold instead of the gun."

"You're serious, aren't you?"

"It's a long story. Treachery inside the Pinkerton Agency and my own stupidity. I'll tell you about it when I'm in a better mood. What troubles me now is that we needed a prisoner out of this slaughter. Nobody here is going to be talking, and I don't know how in the hell we'd track these men across this prairie. Looked to me like they were heading south, and eventually you hit rough country down that way—hills, draws, canyons and the like."

Audra said, "We've got a prisoner. He should be waking up by now. Clay put him out for a bit. We've got a cowboy friend watching after him in the second passenger car."

"I don't want to leave the gold unguarded in case that outfit would double back. Think you two can get the man back here to chat a bit? Might not hurt for him to meet up with his friends, anyhow. Why don't you ask your cowboy friend if he knows anything about this country? If he does, see if he'd be willing to come back and talk with us."

Audra said, "Clay, why don't you go on ahead? I'd like to stop at the cattle car where I've got my gear stored and slip into my riding britches and boots. My dress wasn't made for this kind of work."

Chapter 23

"DARB, WE CAN'T go off chasing after that gang and leave the gold unguarded," Trace said, sitting on the coffin just inside the boxcar while they waited for their partners to return with the prisoner. "We're going to have to split up. Problem is, we were cooped up in this boxcar, and I don't know where the hell we're at."

Darby stood outside, hat pulled low on her forehead to keep it from escaping in the dry Kansas wind, her long, golden hair fluttering about her neck and face. "Audra and Clay should know. We've got to get the gold to a bank vault someplace. I think you and I should head after the Blue Bandanas and try to locate the hideout and leave Audra and Clay to look after the gold."

"Two of us won't be able to take on what's left of the gang. Our reports said they seem to operate with two different crews. If that's the case, we chewed one of them up pretty good today, but that still leaves a good number of men dug in on their own ground."

Darby countered, "But if we learn the girl's there, we might be able to get her out. Or we can keep the gang busy until Audra and Clay show up."

Trace was still troubled by the number of gang members they could potentially encounter. No sense speculating. They needed to talk to the prisoner, he thought, a moment before Clay and Audra appeared with a young man, hands cuffed behind his back, who staggered ahead of them, prodded by Clay's rifle barrel. The fair complexioned, shaggy-haired captive displayed an angry blood-dripping gash carved through an egg-sized knot above his right ear. The dazed look on his face suggested he was short of recovery from the blow Clay had rendered.

A lean, taciturn-faced man followed Clay and Audra, and his attire said cowhand or cattleman, but the dark eyes that appraised the scattering of corpses without any apparent unease suggested he was not uninitiated to violent death. Ex-soldier, perhaps? The prisoner stumbled and went to his knees.

Trace said, "Just put him down there."

Clay helped the man to a spot on the ground, and Trace dropped out of the boxcar. He looked at the cowboy and extended his hand, "I'm Trace Crockett." He nodded toward Darby. "This is my wife, Darby. You've probably been told, we're all operatives for the Pinkerton National Detective Agency."

The cowboy stepped up and returned a firm grip. "Ted Colmes. My pleasure. I just hopped the train fresh from a cattle drive to Denver. I was headed to Dodge City to see if I might find cow work there. Or something else up my line."

"What else is up your line?"

"What ain't might be easier. Been a buffalo hunter, Army scout, sheriff's deputy, bounty hunter—that's for a start." His lips parted just a bit to show a wry smile. "Always on the right side of the law, or not too far on the other."

"Stick around a bit. We might have some temporary work for you."

"Don't look like I'm going anyplace soon."

Trace sat down in front of the prisoner, crossing his legs Indian style. He noticed that the kid's eyes were fastened on the corpses of his late comrades. Good.

"Young man," Trace said. "Time to talk."

He turned his head toward Trace. "Got nothin' to say."

"What's your name?" Trace asked.

The prisoner hesitated. "I go by Jim-Bob. Last name's Hansen."

"That's a start. Now, I don't have time to waste. I'll start the talking. When I get done, if you've still got nothing to stay, we'll string you up and look for our answers elsewhere."

"String me up? Hang me? You can't do that. Ain't legal."

"Quickest way to deal with you. We don't have time to track down a sheriff or marshal. Now listen. By my count, seven of your friends died today trying to take what wasn't theirs. You were in the car where an innocent man died. At the least, you were an accomplice to that killing. That's likely enough for hanging. Or it puts you in Lansing Prison till you're gumming your food. That's just for this job. I've got a hunch you've been on others. Do you think your old friends won't try to pin any other killings on you?"

"I never kilt nobody. Never."

"Doesn't matter. Somebody else will likely say you did to save his own hide. Do you really think your so-called friends wouldn't do that? I don't think you're that stupid."

"What happens if I tell you what I know?"

"If you tell us the truth and everything you know, we'll tell the law how you helped us and ask that you be charged with only one count of robbery. That could have you out of prison in five years. You can't be more than twenty. You would still be a young man. I can't promise anything except we'd try to help you."

Jim-Bob sighed. His eyes were tear-filled, and Trace could see that the seriousness of the young man's dilemma was sinking in. He did not sense that Jim-Bob was a cold-blooded killer. More likely he was a lost sheep, short on education or marketable skills, and fell in with the wrong crowd. The lure of quick and easy money came next. Too slow on the brain trigger to consider the risks, let alone the moral implications.

"What do you want to know?" Jim-Bob asked.

"Who's the top dog of the Blue Bandana outfit?"

Jim-Bob shrugged. "Nobody knows. Well, I suppose Bart Wince does. He gives all the orders, but he leaves the canyon to see some higher up that gives him the word. Usually gone near a week to meet up with somebody and get back. Don't know where or who."

"You mentioned a canyon. That's your hideout?"

"Yeah. They call it Copperhead Canyon 'cause of the snakes. Copperheads by the buckets up there in the rocks. Gotta watch your step for damn sure."

Trace didn't like the sound of that. The only thing he feared more than heights were snakes—any kind, poisonous or not. He'd willingly walk a mile to bypass one on a trail, if that's what it took. Handling one was unthinkable. He wondered if he had ever mentioned his ir-rational fear to Darby. He thought not, although she was aware of his dislike of heights.

"Where is this canyon?"

"Ever hear of No Man's Land?"

"Yes. I've been there."

"Well, I don't know how it all comes together, but the canyon's at the west end of that country. I guess Kansas and Texas and Colorado—even New Mexico Territory all touch No Man's Land someplace. Indian Territory, too."

He gave Jim-Bob credit. He had his geography right. West end. That still covers a lot of territory. "Do you cross the Cimarron to get there from the north?"

"Yeah. That's the one. Not deep during dry times. Sandy bottom. Gotta watch for quicksand. Big river south not too many miles. Ain't traveled that way much."

Ted Colmes spoke. "The Beaver River, also known as the North Canadian by some. I been in that country dur-ing my scouting days. Can I ask a question?"

Trace said, "Help yourself."

"You ever seen a big mesa in that area? A low moun-tain. Black rocks."

Jim-Bob said, "Think I know what you're talking of. Never up there. Can see it when you're above the canyon and to the north and west. Passed that way coming from a bank job up in Colorado. Looks sort of like the Rockies from where we was, passing on the east some miles away."

Colmes said, "We called it the black mesa. I was tracking Cheyenne headed for Indian Territory in those days. Wasn't much more than a kid then. Got my bellyful of the Army that fall and winter."

Darby asked, "You can find this black mesa?"

"Hard to miss if you're in the general neighborhood," Colmes said.

Trace turned back to Jim-Bob. "We're looking for a girl."

"Maddie, she said her name was."

"Then you saw her."

"Yeah, I saw her."

"Is she okay?"

"When we left, she was at the canyon. Rumor was Bart wanted to trade her for money. Guess her old man's got money. With the railroad. Bax—he's our crew boss—he don't think they'll do it. She's seen everybody. Knows the hideout. Thinks they'll have to kill her. I didn't want no part of that. Liked her. Felt bad for her. Pretty thing, but she was tougher than a boot. Moon Parker took her— know what I mean? Couple of times. She cussed him out.

Never heard some of them words before, and that's saying something. Never seen her cry once."

Darby asked, her voice shaky, "He raped her?"

Jim-Bob looked down at his hands as if studying something there and mumbled, "Yeah, guess that's the word. I tried to stop him. I tried, but he said he'd kill me if I didn't get back. Said I could have her when he was done. But I didn't do it, I swear. I wouldn't."

The kid was convincing, but Trace just hoped they had a chance to find out the truth. "Where do they keep her?"

"When we rode out, she was bunked in a cabin by her lonesome. Sort of off by itself on lower ground near the west end of the canyon. North of the stream what cuts through there. But they got a guard posted outside. 'Course, where would she go anyhow? That's damn rough country out there. No way she'd find her way out if she made a run for it. But I couldn't swear she's still there. Anything could have happened by now, and when Bart Wince finds out about today, I wouldn't bet on nothing."

"Then we've got work to do," Trace said.

Chapter 24

THEY REMOVED THE handcuffs and cinched Jim-Bob Hansen's hands loosely behind his back and hitched the rope end to a low ladder rung on the boxcar. Trace wasn't concerned about him trying to make a break and run. Where would he go? Besides, the kid was scared as a whipped pup and trying to make friends now, his tongue loose as an erupting geyser, almost throwing out more information than they could digest. They had gotten lucky with their captive and taken someone with virtually no reluctance to change sides.

Jim-Bob furnished rough directions to the canyon, admitting he wasn't certain he could find the place on his own. He told them he was just glad to be alive. The Blue Bandanas did not leave gang members behind alive. Wounded who could not ride were summarily executed.

Trace gathered the detectives and Colmes near the boxcar opening and directed his first remarks to Colmes. "If you're looking for work, Ted, our agency will pay you five dollars a day to help us on this job, plus you can collect reward money on any of the outlaws that might have paper out on them."

Colmes's eyes widened, "That's a lot of money without any rewards. You're serious?"

"I'm serious."

"Count me in."

"Good. Now, Darb and I made this trip in a boxcar. We don't know where the hell we're at. Can you tell us?"

Colmes said, "Sure. You're less than ten miles west of Garden City. Decent sized town. Right down the tracks."

"Banks?"

"Yep. I been there. Had two about a year ago."

"Law?"

"Sheriff and at least two deputies."

"I'm sure it's got an undertaker."

"Yeah. One that I know of. I think he does barbering, too, and pulls a few teeth on the side."

"Okay," Trace said, turning to Darby. "How much cash you got stashed?"

"A thousand dollars. I put the rest of the Pinkerton advance in the Manhattan Bank."

"And Audra has bank authorization?"

"Yes. She can send a wire for more, if needed."

"We're probably stuck for burial costs, and the bank will want fees for holding the gold. Here's what I propose. Tell me if it doesn't make sense. Audra will take the cash and ride on to Garden City and report what happened to the railroad depot and the sheriff. Tell the sheriff there's a prisoner for him to pick up. We can check with the engineer or conductor to see if they have special contacts or instructions for getting a crew out to patch the tracks."

Audra said, "We've got some extra horses the outlaws left behind, a few tied and some running loose. I say Ted takes his pick, and then if the conductor or engineer or somebody wants to take one and ride with me, he can talk to the folks at the depot or send wires or whatever he's got to do. They'll have to get the passengers to Garden City and put them up till the train can move on."

"What about the gold?" Darby asked.

"Audra will arrange for a team, driver, and wagon to come out and pick that up after she makes arrangements for safekeeping with a bank," Trace said. "Put it in the undertaker's hands to transport the bodies. Tell him we've got seven would-be robbers and a passenger."

Audra said, "The dead passenger's brother is here. I'll tell him an undertaker will be coming out, and he can be thinking about arrangements. I don't know where the gentlemen were from, or if they were headed home or just starting on a visit."

Colmes said, "I'd like photographs of the deceased outlaws and Mister Hansen here. I think the undertaker's in that business, too."

Trace said, "Add that to our tab, too, Audra." That earned him an elbow in the ribs from Darby. He continued, "I'd like Clay and Ted to stay here and guard the gold. I don't expect more trouble, but you never know. When Audra returns, I'd like the three of you to accompany the gold to the bank. Don't leave it till a bank officer has receipted for the bullion."

Darby said, "We need to notify Pink about what's happened and give him a hint about what we're up to."

"And," Trace added, "about the corruption in the Denver office. You're the expert with the weasel words. Do you want to write up a message for Audra to send?"

"I'm not sure whether I just got a compliment or not. But, yes, I'll do that. You'd tell him more than he needs to know."

"See, that's what I meant."

Darby turned and walked away to retrieve her pencil and writing paper that were with her gear in the cattle car.

Clay had been silent during all the discussion, but Trace had come to understand that was just his way. He was a man careful with his words, one of those rare persons who had discovered one learns more when his own lips aren't flapping.

Now, he spoke. "Trace, you haven't said what you and Darby are going to be doing. I'm guessing you're going to try tracking what's left of the Blue Bandana bunch?"

"Yes, we're going to get our gear and mounts and saddle up in a few minutes. With Jim-Bob's directions we can get in the vicinity even if we don't pick up a trail someplace. I did some tracking during the Red River War. I'm not the best, but I'm not the worst either. I'm looking to find the south and east side of this canyon."

"And when we're done with delivering the gold?"

"Then I'm hoping you'll find us. Ted sounds like he knows his way around that country." He turned to Colmes. "I'm thinking you might try to locate this Copperhead Canyon from the black mesa area you mentioned, so we'd be working from different directions. Does that make sense?"

"As much as anything"

Trace pulled his watch from his trouser pocket. "Watch says twelve-forty five. You won't be finished in town till after dark, so there's no sense in you heading out from Garden City till morning. Stay longer if that's what it takes to secure the gold and get the other business taken care of. We'll hope to find each other in No Man's Land. I don't think we can foresee enough to plan any more than we have."

Chapter 25

TRACE AND DARBY rode their horses at an easy lope south toward a sea of rolling prairie grasses, Trace astride his big buckskin stallion, Atlas, and Darby mounted on the blood bay gelding she had dubbed "Cinnamon" for the color of its coat. She had been warned by horsemen not to name a mount, because the act cemented a bond that made it more difficult to sell or trade an animal when good sense dictated it was time. It didn't matter. She and Cinnamon were "till death do us part" companions. Fortunately, Trace shared her outlook about some of his own critters and had named his own mount and did not tease her about it.

They had been riding for better than an hour, and the train was far behind them and out of sight now. They had not brought a pack horse with them on the train journey out of concern that the extra animal would slow their pace. Darby was having second thoughts about that decision. Aside from their weapons and canteens, they carried bedrolls and their separate buffalo skin "possible sacks" that carried items each considered indispensable for personal use. A small kettle was suspended from Trace's saddle, and a canvas bag that carried deer and beef jerky he had brought from home and biscuits picked up at a Denver bakery was hitched to the bedroll behind the saddle.

Darby had stuffed a mystery bag of vittles into her possible sack. Clay had collected some food from the railroad dining car and handed the bag to her just before they departed, but she worried they were not adequately provisioned. She tended to defer to Trace when it came to survival in the wilderness, however. Her history as an Irish schoolteacher from Boston had not granted her credentials to question his judgment on such matters.

They had spoken little since departure, and though she did not mind comfortable silences, she was getting curious about Trace's thinking—and she could sense that he had some ideas churning in his head. She edged her gelding closer to Trace's buckskin. "Are you going to share your thoughts?" she asked.

Trace nodded toward a scattering of cottonwoods off to the west, perhaps a quarter of a mile distant. "Bet there's water near the trees. Let's head over there and take a rest, give the horses a good drink. And we can talk. Maybe see what's in that bag Clay gave you."

"Let's go."

When they reached the trees, Darby was not surprised to see that they lined a clear creek that tumbled over a rocky bed. A nice stand of shortgrass carpeted the area along the creek banks, so they were able to stake the horses out in the shade beneath the trees after letting the animals drink their fill. They sat down beneath the obviously senior of several cottonwoods, leaning their backs against the tree trunk. Darby opened the paper bag Clay had given her.

"Sliced beef sandwiches. Four of them."

"Two for tonight's supper," Trace said. "The others for tomorrow noon. We can save our other supplies for when things get leaner. Anything else?"

"Looks like a half dozen oatmeal cookies. Same of shortbread strips and four apples."

"What would you think of a cookie and apple apiece right now? Tide us over to suppertime. It's after three o'clock. I'm thinking we'll ride till near sundown."

She held the sack out. "Help yourself."

As they ate, Trace explained what he had in mind. "Did you see the road apples on the trail?"

"Yes. Do you think they're from the Blue Bandana horses?"

"Likely. Droppings look like today's business. Picked up the first sign no more than a mile south of the train. We aren't more than a few hours behind them."

"But we don't want to catch up anyway, do we?"

"I think we'd rather have them lead us to this Copperhead Canyon. But I'd like to close the gap some. So far, we've had easy going, but you'll recall from our last visit to No Man's Land, that the country gets rougher as we move south. We aren't that much further west, so I don't think we can look for anything much different, and from what Colmes said, it might be worse."

"At least it's not storming. No floods or tornados."

"Yet."

"Mister Optimism."

"I'm thinking our friends won't stray far from this creek for a spell. Water supply, wooded spots for setting up camp or hiding out, if need be. That would work for us, too. Sooner or later, this creek's going to send its water to the Cimarron, so this trail would be consistent with what Jim-Bob Hansen told us. One thing I'm concerned about, though."

"What's that?"

"They don't seem to be trying to hide their trail at all. It's been dry, and the ground's hard most places, but they don't make any effort to avoid loose dirt or sand they come across. Either they're darned confident they're not being followed, or they want us on their trail."

"You're thinking possible ambush?"

"Can't rule it out. I don't think we're that vulnerable right now. It would be hard to set up something in the open prairie we're in, but when we ride into hill country, we'd better keep our eyes open."

Later, Darby saw a sod house off the trail some hundred yards distant. It appeared several men were working on a frame structure nearby. "I wonder if they've seen anything?" she mused.

"Can't hurt to ask. Looks like homesteaders. I noticed some other dugouts and a few log homes in the distance. I'd guess there are some small towns springing up to serve these folks."

They reined east and trotted their mounts toward the site of the activity. Darby noted a winding wagon path led to the opposite side of the property and connected to a ribbon of dirt that might pass for a road. Cornfields, half dried up but with some salvageable crop, lined the wagon ruts leading away from the house. As they approached, a blond-bearded man wearing a straw hat and bib overalls stepped off a ladder and picked up a shotgun leaning against a nearby wheelbarrow. Trace and Darby slowed the horses, and Trace offered a friendly wave.

"Howdy," Trace said. "Sorry to interrupt your work. My name's Trace Crockett." He nodded toward Darby. "This is my wife Darby." His right thumb pointed toward the Pinkerton badge pinned to the left breast of his shirt. "We're Pinkerton agents. Could I step down and ask a few questions?"

The man relaxed his grip on the shotgun but did not put it aside. Darby noticed that an elderly man and a boy not more than sixteen were watching warily through the window spaces of the as-yet unsided, single-story house. She suspected the old man, and possibly the boy, secreted weapons out of the visitors' sight.

He nodded his approval. "Ja, es ist gut. Ich bin Johann Gerhardt. Over there are my son and father." He gestured toward the silent observers.

Darby noticed that the man, whom she guessed to be in his late thirties, spoke English with only a trace of an accent. She suspected the German phraseology was habit ingrained from conversing with his father, who was probably more comfortable with his native tongue. She glanced toward the sod house and saw a pretty woman with hair as blonde as her own standing in the doorway with two small girls at her side and a boy peering out wide-eyed from behind her skirt. Darby smiled at her and received a friendly smile back.

Trace dismounted. "We're looking for some men who tried to rob a train. They're called the Blue Bandana Gang. I'm guessing there are four. We want to be certain we're tracking the right people."

"Ja. Four. They came here. When they saw we had guns, they turned away and left. They wore the blue bandanas. From the way he sat in the saddle, I think one man was wounded. Bad, maybe. We would have helped him, taken him in even. Meine Frau, Greta, is good with the sick and wounded. We would not turn such a man away, but his friends would have been made to put their weapons down."

"They would not have taken kindly to that," Trace said. "Where are we at? We don't have a map. We expect to follow these men to a hideout in No Man's Land between the Cimarron and Beaver Rivers."

"I do not know the Beaver River, but the North Loup of the Cimarron River is about twenty miles southwest of here. Or you can go southwest about fifteen miles to Ulysses and connect to the river there. That is the furthest point the Cimarron comes into Kansas. It comes northeast from No Man's Land to Ulysses and then goes back southeast to No Man's Land from there. We get most all our supplies out of Ulysses. It's an overnight trip with buckboard and team. A hard day there and back with horse and pack mule."

"That helps. We won't decide until we see where their trail takes us, or we lose it."

"South, you are about an hour away from hill country and then badlands. Your trail will not be so good there. And, except from a hilltop, you will not see far in front of you."

Trace said, "Thanks, Mister Gerhardt. You've been very helpful."

Darby plunged her fingers into her possible bag and dug out two double eagles. She nudged Cinnamon forward. "Please accept this," she said, bending from her saddle and handing the coins to the German farmer.

He took the coins and opened his hand. He looked up at Darby and started shaking his head. "Nein. No. That is too much."

"You must take it. I would be offended otherwise."

"Gott segne dich. God bless you."

Trace shook the flustered man's hand and mounted Atlas. "Thanks for taking the time to give us the information. Goodbye."

"Auf viedersehen, friend. We wish you a safe journey."

"Thanks. We may need that."

As they rode back to the trail, Trace said, "You do know that forty bucks was a fortune to that man. Farmers never have extra cash. They can live high on the hog for two or three months with that kind of money. Where's Miss Skinflint, the woman I married?"

"I know how hard life is for the homesteaders. I taught some of their kids when I was teaching at the school near Dodge City. They work their fingers to the bone trying to make a better life for their kids. Sometimes, they're lucky to get a crop every two or three years. A lot of them starve out. Those folks weren't building an extravagant house. Just a place to get off the dirt floor. It doesn't hurt for us to spread a little hope."

He sidled the buckskin up next to the blood bay and leaned out and stretched his arm about her waist and squeezed gently. "I wasn't complaining, Love. I'm glad you did it. You just never stop surprising me, that's all. One of a ton of reasons I love you so much." His eyes met hers, and she could see the laughter there.

As they moved back onto the trail, Trace said, "How about we set up camp as soon as we see the hill country coming on?"

"I thought you wanted to ride till dusk."

"Don't want to move into the hills when dark's setting in. Maybe we can hit the bedrolls soon and get an early start."

"I thought bedrolls had something to do with it," she teased. "Early start on what?"

"I suppose you're going to say my thoughts are unprofessional."

"Well, they're certainly close to it. But we do have responsibilities to our marriage, too."

"That's the kind of talk I like to hear."

She knew that she'd already lost the battle, if there had even been one. Whenever those smoke-gray eyes fastened on hers, her brain always turned south.

Chapter 26

TRACE AND DARBY slowed their mounts when they left the tablelands behind the next morning, and their path began to narrow and twist between grass-cloaked ridges and knolls. The soil here was turning gritty and rockier, Trace observed, the hoofprints fading. Then he caught a glimpse of something that interested him on the trail ahead, and he reined in the buckskin stallion. Darby rode up beside him.

"What is it?" she asked.

"Not sure." He dismounted, handed Darby the buckskin's reins and stepped a few paces forward to the area that had grabbed his attention. He knelt on one knee and studied the rocky and gravelly path that ran no more than ten feet wide between the hillocks at this juncture. A mound of partially mashed horse turds marked the passage of the outlaws here, but the mass of dried blood and the disturbances in the ground wrote the story he was trying to read.

Beneath the brown, caked blood were splotches of sticky, red sediment, telling him that not more than a few hours had passed since the riders paused at this place. The quantity of blood residue suggested someone had bled out here. He cast his eyes about and locked on to the remainder of the story. Blood in the matted grass that led up the gradual slope of the knoll, where a man's boot heels had carved a trail like sled runners as his body was drug to the top.

Darby dismounted now, and clutching the horses' reins, moved up behind him. "Blood?"

"Yep. I think the wounded man died here and they drug him up the hill. I'm going to take a look."

Trace stood and headed up the incline, following the blood and boot trail to the knoll's top, where the ground leveled off again. He peered over the other side and saw the crumpled corpse that had evidently been tossed over the edge, where it had rolled down the slope and landed in a shallow gully at the base of the hillock. Trace scrambled down the rugged grade, stumbling and nearly losing his footing once.

When he reached the body, he rolled it over, so he could examine the dead man. Chest wound. No chance without a doc. The gunshot wound in the temple would not have been inflicted by Pinkerton operatives. He could not have ridden ten feet with that one. A Blue Bandana comrade fired that shot. Trace would have buried the man if he had carried a shovel with his gear. But he had none, so he left the body for the scavengers that would move in soon enough.

Darby looked at him questioningly when he returned.

"The wounded man is now dead," he said. "They dropped him on the other side of the rise. One of his own finished him off with a bullet in the head. I suppose he was slowing them down, and they didn't want to chance his talking. I don't think they're more than an hour ahead of us and probably know we're on the hunt. We may want to slow our pace a bit."

"So we just leave him?"

"No choice. Another young fella, like Jim-Bob. Saw a chance for easy money. No conscience troubling him. He deserved his end, but it's still sad. We've always had a certain number of this kind in the world. Always will."

Darby put her foot in the stirrup and swung into her saddle. "Let's get out of here."

A half hour later, Darby said. "Your eyes must be better than mine because I'm not seeing any tracks. And these hills all look alike. I'm lost."

"I'm not seeing much, but I can tell you they split up about fifty feet back. A single rider took a west fork between the ridges back there. The other two are ahead of us, making no effort to hide their trail. Look to your left at the edge of the trail. You'll see softer dirt that's silted down from the slopes. They're deliberately riding there to leave some sign."

"They want us to find them?"

"They want us to follow."

"They're setting up the ambush, aren't they?"

"I'd say so."

"Why don't you tell me what you're planning?"

"Do you mind waiting again? I'd like to track the lone rider."

"Why don't I just keep riding. Very slowly. Now that I can see the tracks, I can go on up the trail and keep any shooter distracted."

"I don't like the idea of using you as a decoy. Too risky."

"Trace, if you hadn't noticed, risk is what Pinkertons do. I'll keep my eyes out and be ready to dive for cover if shooting starts."

"Okay. I don't like it. But waiting isn't my game either. Go ahead but keep your head low."

Trace wheeled the buckskin around and backtracked to where the lone outlaw had forked off the main trail. Darby nudged her blood bay forward at a walking pace.

The tracking demanded no great skill, Trace thought. The trail was not generally used for rider and horse travel. It was less than half the width of the main trail and the main path narrow and worn, more likely a route for deer and other wild creatures. Fragments of shooed hoof prints were not difficult for his eyes to pick up, and it was obvious the rider was angling for higher ground into some sandstone bluffs that loomed over the surrounding low and rolling hills. It was a natural spot for ambush, craggy stone hiding spots overlooking the main trail and a panoramic view of the trail. He cringed at the thought of Darby riding into that trap and was struck with an urgency to ferret out the would-be assassin.

As he neared the bluffs, he saw the ambusher's horse hitched to a spindly cedar clinging to the base and noted the path that wound upward some fifty feet into rocks. He dismounted, tying his own mount to another cedar and pulled his Sharps from the saddle scabbard. He loaded the gun, which was an 1874 model used by the military during the Indian wars. It had range and power and had been favored by many buffalo hunters. There were more efficient rifles in terms of firing speed. The Henry and Winchester had an edge when it came to loading and chambering, but he still had an affinity for his Sharps.

His first thought was to head up the path that led to the top of the bluffs, but he decided his disadvantage would be too great. He could not see the gunman, but if the man saw him first, Trace had no place to take cover. He would make a target a child could take down. He decided to walk around the base of the bluffs which rose like a giant, chipped molar from the earth, running at least a hundred feet from northeasterly to southwesterly and about half that distance in width. To gain a better shooting angle, he walked half way up a nearby hillock, where he found a cluster of sandstone boulders that had doubtless belonged to the bluffs before the ravages of time and, perhaps a storm, had loosened their bonding and propelled them off their perch.

From here, he saw a splash of red move in the rocks above, a man's shirt, he assumed. He decided he would fire a few shots in that direction, divert the man's attention from Darby's course and draw him into exposing his position. He found a comfortable spot among the stones, sat down and braced himself against a large boulder. He started to aim the Sharps in the direction he had seen the movement but froze when two rifle shots cracked and broke the morning calm.

His heart raced at the thought that Darby might be on the receiving end of the bullets. Then the bushwhacker, a tall, skinny man, emerged from behind his stone fortress and headed for the path that would take him to his horse. He stopped suddenly when he saw Trace, raised his rifle to fire, when the Sharps roared and drove lead into the bushwhacker's chest. Before he toppled over, another bullet tore into his gut, and he went off the pathway, sliding down a slope of loose stones before catapulting over the sheer cliff and landing on the ground not more than thirty feet from Trace.

Trace did not need to check the shooter's condition. He got up and raced for the outlaw's chestnut gelding, unhitched the horse and led it to his stallion. He subdued his rising panic and considered his options for returning to the main trail, deciding that rather than backtracking, he would take the southwesterly route around the bluffs and then locate the trail and angle back toward Darby.

Moments later, he broke around the bluffs, encouraged to find the trail had twisted in his direction. The hills blocked his view, however, and he saw no sign of his wife. She could not have been far away, he thought, to come within the bushwhacker's sight and range. It was like working his way through a maze in this stretch of hill country, and the minutes seemed like hours until he reined the buckskin around a sharp turn in the trail and encountered a Winchester pointed at his midsection.

Chapter 27

DARBY LOWERED THE rifle when she saw that the rider was Trace. "You scared the pee out of me," she said.

"I was afraid you'd been shot. I heard two shots, and the bushwhacker stepped out like he thought he hit you."

If she did not know better, she would have sworn she saw tears glazing Trace's eyes when he dismounted. He walked over to her, pulled her into his arms and just held her tightly, saying nothing and still saying everything. She squeezed him before easing back.

Darby said, "There wasn't much doubt where the guy would be waiting, so I kept my eyes on the bluffs. When I saw a flash off metal in the sunlight, I started to slide off Cinnamon, and when the rifle cracked, I just kept sliding, landed on my butt, rolled over and played possum. I don't know how close the first shot was, but it must have been the second that lodged in my saddle. After I heard the other shots, I guessed you were busy, so I got up and chased Cinnamon down the backtrail. He didn't go far. He was waiting." She paused, "You did take the ambusher down, didn't you?"

Trace nodded, "Yeah, I took him down."

"I really didn't need to ask since you brought back another horse."

"I guess an extra won't hurt in case one comes up lame or needs a rest."

"Our last assignment we ended up with a herd of orphaned horses."

"The chestnut might not be the last on this trip," Trace said. "You ready to move on?"

"I'm ready."

They mounted and moved on to search for the trail of the two remaining riders. An hour later, they still had not found any sign of the pursued.

"It's like something swooped down, picked them up and carried them off," Darby said.

"Somewhere, they broke off the trail," Trace said. "We're wasting time. Chances are they've reached the Cimarron and crossed by now. Let's stop and enjoy a gourmet meal of dried biscuits and jerky and then head south for the Cimarron. Maybe we can pick up their trail on the other side."

"We can't follow the river, though. If we go northwest along its course, we'd end up going almost backwards into Kansas till we reached Ulysses."

"No, after we cross the Cimarron, we keep going south till we hit the Beaver River and follow that west across No Man's Land. If Jim-Bob wasn't lying, that would get us in the vicinity of the Copperhead Canyon hideout."

Chapter 28

DARKNESS HAD CAST its shroud over the little town of Garden City, Kansas by the time the train passengers and crew were transported by wagons and lodged in the two hotels. On her first trip to town Audra had made reservations for rooms at "Grandma's Beds & Eats" for Clay, Colmes and herself, but they had missed supper at the boarding house by the time they reached Garden City with the gold-filled coffin and deposited the treasure in the vault at the Kansas State Bank.

The white-haired, kindly bank president and a young clerk had remained at the bank long after hours to receive the gold and were somewhat befuddled when they discovered that the bullion was packed in a coffin. They gamely assisted the buckboard driver from the livery and the two male detectives with carrying the cargo into the bank vault. Audra had tried to help, but Colmes said it was man's work. Small as she was, Audra still figured she could handle her share of the load better than the puny, fuzzy-cheeked clerk, but she did not care. She knew that men needed to feel superior about such things. Too bad so many were short on brains, John Trace Crockett and Clayton Sibley being among the exceptions.

After the coffin was set in the vault, Colmes excused himself to meet up with the undertaker, who would be working this night, too, on two wagonloads of corpses that had been hauled back from the disabled train. Colmes wanted to help photograph the Blue Bandana bodies and locate identifying marks to support claims to any rewards. Sheriff Norbert Anderson, a huskily built, middle-aged man with a brushy, blond moustache, had agreed to assist with processing any reward claims. The ruddy-faced Swede seemed to be a competent, efficient man, and his two young deputies treated him with respect, a clue that he was a man in charge of his domain. Audra was comfortable leaving Jim-Bob Hansen in the sheriff's custody.

Audra and Clay watched now as the bank president and clerk inventoried the gold bullion for the receipt Audra had requested.

"Step out here with me," Audra said softly to Clay as she headed for the opening to the walk-in vault.

When Clay joined her, she said, "I don't think they're going anywhere with the gold, and I haven't had a chance to talk with you alone."

"You've been busy, Audra. All the arrangements have been on your shoulders. I would have stepped up more, but your colleagues put a woman and a colored man in charge of getting things done here. We're dealing with mostly white men, and some may be leery of working with a woman. But more are wary of a dark-skinned fella—Negro, Indian or whatever. Not whining. Just a fact. And you've done just fine. I'm here to cover your back. If you want me to handle anything, just say so."

She thought that was about the longest speech she had heard from this quiet, calm man. "Thank you, Clay. I'm grateful to have you on my side." She pulled a folded sheet of paper from her pocket. "I'd intended to show you this earlier, the message Darby had me wire to Allan Pinkerton at the Chicago office." She unfolded the sheet and handed it to Clay.

He read the message aloud, "Gold secure. Continuing mission. Snakes in Colorado Pinkerton office. Cromwell and one other. Darby Crockett." Clay returned the paper. "That should get his attention."

"Yeah," Audra said, "Darby told me somebody would be arranging train connections for Denver before the boss read the message a second time. Now, we need to talk about tomorrow. We should have our business finished here tonight. We need to head out at sunrise. I traded two of the extra horses we picked up from the outlaws to the livery man for a good pack mule and supplies on a list I gave him. He's to have the supplies stacked at the stable when we get there in the morning. With three of us, we need a pack animal. It might slow us some, but not that much."

"You think of everything, don't you?"

"There's likely something I forgot. But there's something I want to ask you."

"Go ahead."

"What's your opinion of Ted Colmes?"

Clay's eyes narrowed and he was silent a moment before he spoke. "I'm slow to judge a man. I've been wrong about a lot of folks in my time. Some turned out better than I first thought. Some turned out worse."

"That's no answer."

"Well, for now I'll say this. I see him as a man of convenient principles. He stays mostly on the right side of the law because he's smart enough to know most don't step across the line without hanging or going to jail. He'd be a good man to have on your side in a fight, and I don't think he'd be a coward. But he's got to have a reason to stick with you. In our case, mostly money. Not a complex man, but like the rest of us, he's got a few ghosts, and maybe a sense of justice, buried somewhere."

"We need his help. He just makes me uneasy."

"He'll do for this assignment. And, remember, I've got your back."

At the boarding house, Grandma Biggs was kind enough to invite Audra and Clay into the kitchen for leftovers, which turned out to be the best meal Audra could remember eating for months. Roast beef, mashed potatoes and gravy, fresh corn, sourdough bread, all finished off with a slice of apple pie. Grandma was a buxom lady with an ever-present smile, and Audra wished she could stay a few days longer to get to know her better. Maybe it had to do with her search for family, all of whom were dead, except for the father who had abandoned her when she was fifteen. Trace and Darby Crockett were family now, but there were no blood ties.

Later, after bidding goodnight to Clay, who occupied the room next to hers, she locked her door and undressed for bed. She had no bedclothes, so she crawled into bed naked, her sleeping preference anyway. Sleep evaded her regardless because her mind was locked on preparations for the journey to No Man's Land and this place called Copperhead Canyon.

She was a fair sketch artist and had been told by others she had an artistic gift. She doubted that, but on the wagon journey from the stalled train to Garden City, based upon conversations with Jim-Bob Hansen and Ted Colmes, she had sketched a rough map of the area south of the Cimarron River. The river apparently ran along the black mesa's southern edge, and she targeted an approximate area where the canyon should be located. She had also marked the location of Ulysses, Kansas at the northernmost fork of the Cimarron River. She estimated a long day's trip to Ulysses and had allowed for supplementing supplies there and purchasing anything she had overlooked.

She was starting to worry whether Colmes would even show up. She had not seen him since he separated from Clay and her at the bank. He had a room across the hall, but she had not heard him come in. She would bet he was gambling or drinking at one of the saloons, probably both. She hoped he would be fit to travel tomorrow. If not, they would leave without him.

Finally, her eyes closed, and she surrendered to a fitful sleep that ended when she was awakened by the loud hammering on her door. Instinctively, she reached for the Derringer on the bedside table and swung her feet out of bed. Audra pulled the top blanket off the mattress and wrapped it about her body, securing the cover with the fingers of one hand and clutching the hidden Derringer in the other. She stepped toward the door.

"Who is it?" she hollered.

"Open the door."

Despite the slurring, she recognized the voice of Ted Colmes. "What do you want?"

"You. I want you. Let me in."

Assuming he wanted to talk, she slipped the bolt from the clasp and opened the door a crack. Colmes slipped a booted foot into the space and slammed his shoulder into the door, sending her stumbling backwards, the blanket slipping momentarily and releasing her ample breasts before she recovered and pulled it snug again.

"You'd better leave now," she said.

"How much for a poke?"

"You're crazy. Get out of here."

His lips parted in a drunken grin. "I know who you are. It's been eating at me since I first saw you. Stone Creek. The Manor. I had some bounty money then, and I wanted the fanciest whore in the place. I paid fifty dollars for a full night and got the best rides of my life. Never forgot it. You was fancied up then, but there ain't no hiding what you got, sweetheart. I seen what's under that blanket once. I want to see it again. I can pay for the fifty-dollar special. An eagle and two doubles."

She did not remember him. There would have been hundreds during six or seven years of whoring. You endured it by keeping the customers faceless, reminding yourself that you were merchandise, erasing the memory when you had earned your pay. Her only unforgettable coupling was the night with Trace Crockett, the last time she had been with a man, and he had not been a customer.

Audra eased the Derringer from beneath the blanket and aimed it at Colmes's chest. "You're a big man, but this is my equalizer. You come near, and you're a dead man. You turn and walk away, and I'll assume the whiskey's been talking tonight. You've still got a job if you show up at the stable at sunrise . . . and if you don't give me anymore trouble. But you try this again, and you'd better kill me, because if you don't, you're a dead man."

"Let me do the killing, Audra. It would be a pleasure."

Clay's voice. She saw now that he had slipped up behind Colmes and apparently pressed a gun to his back.

The grin on Colmes's face had disappeared, and he raised his hands in surrender. "Don't want no trouble, ma'am. Like you said, I must've drunk a mite much tonight. I made a mistake. Let me stay on. You Pinkertons will be needing me in No Man's Land."

Clay asked, "What do you want me to do, Audra?"

"Relieve him of his Colt. Give it back if he shows up for work tomorrow."

Clay slipped the Colt from Colmes's holster, and then clutched his shoulder and whipped him around, so the two men faced each other. Audra saw a fury in Clay's dark eyes that made her tremble and for a moment doubted Colmes would live to see the sunrise.

Suddenly, Clay's usual calm returned, and she saw the tension in the naked muscular arms and shoulders relax. "Go," he said softly, stepping aside as Colmes staggered past him and headed across the hallway to his own room.

"Will you be alright?" Clay asked her.

She felt strange, standing in front of him, naked underneath her blanket, no more than six feet distant from the magnificent specimen of manhood, clad only in his undershorts. His eyes were kind now, genuinely concerned, she sensed.

"Yes, thank you." She had to ask him. "You heard what Colmes said?"

He shook his head negatively. "I heard nothing." He stood there, a pistol in each hand and his eyes fastened on hers.

She always thought of herself as an eye reader, but his defied reading now. All she saw was what seemed to be a deep sadness. "I'll be fine now," Audra said.

Clay said, "I'll see you in the morning, then, when I'm more presentable. Grandma said she'd have coffee and cinnamon buns in the dining room and a sack full to take with us." Clay turned and walked out, closing the door behind him.

She put the deadbolt in place, returned the Derringer to the table and spread the blanket back on her bed. She stretched like a cat and crawled beneath the sheets again. She lay there, replaying the incident in her mind. She could not excuse Colmes's behavior. She had never looked upon drunkenness as an excuse for any unseemly conduct. Trust of the man would come with reservations henceforth. What troubled her most was her history with the man, the night or nights she could not recall. She knew that from now on, he would see her as the ex-prostitute, the woman whose body he had pleasured himself with. In his mind's eye, he would always see her naked and available for a price. How many others were there that she might encounter someplace who would remember a night with her?

And Clay had heard. He had lied about that. But, thank God, she had seen no judgment in his eyes. She more than liked this man, and when he had stood half-naked in the room just moments earlier, she had been struck by a desire that only one other man had summoned. It gave her hope that perhaps someday she would have feelings for a man that were natural and right. But for now, she reminded herself, she was a Pinkerton agent. She had snatched a second chance at life and started down a new trail, and she darned well intended to finish it.

Chapter 29

MADDIE SANFORD HAD found her way back to where she had stashed her robe and bag. She quickly took inventory of her possessions. She had the buffalo robe, the Winchester, and a fair amount of ammunition, also the little pot, some lucifers, Minnie's penknife, her half of the scissors-knife, two canteens and the rope Minnie had insisted on bringing. It occurred to her now that all the items they had escaped with had ended up in the bag Minnie left behind, more confirmation her friend never expected to meet up with her again.

She turned north toward what she thought of as the black mountain. She kept an eye out for the scum called Moon. She at once feared the young man and itched to kill him like the animal he was. It was a foreign feeling to her, this desire to kill someone. Was this how outlaws and gunfighters came to be? She loaded up her gear. She had no food, but she had been told by her father a person could live for days without food. Water was the indispensable.

From the location of the sun, Maddie guessed it was mid-afternoon. She was tired but not exhausted and decided to press ahead and hope she might find a suitable place for the night. She wanted to stay well ahead of Moon if he had not given up pursuit. She did not know how badly he had been injured by Minnie's blade, but she hoped he had been damaged enough to abandon the chase. She feared, however, that his altercation with Minnie might have simply left him more resolved. She could take nothing for granted.

She searched the outline of the mountain in the distance, searching for a peak to focus on, but finding none, settled on what appeared to be a skunk's stripe of near white that split the mass, a fissure or opening in the stone, she speculated. She would use that as her private compass bearing to avoid disorientation, a tip she had picked up from Minnie. She had learned so much, she thought, during her few days with that supposedly uneducated woman. She would never see people through the same eyes again.

She found the terrain increasingly desert-like as she walked toward the dark shadow that loomed like a ghost on the horizon, white, billowy clouds hanging over the flat top like a crown. A clear, azure sky and blinding sun had brightened her journey so far, but the destination hinted that another world lay ahead. For now, however, she threaded through iron-red dunes and strange rock formations erupting from the earth, random clusters of stone that had no visible source. She recognized the cholla cactuses and yucca and the occasional juniper and cedar, but most of the plant life was foreign to her.

The wildlife she saw, aside from several rattlesnakes sunning in the rocks, consisted mostly of lizards of assorted sizes and colors skittering across the red, parched earth or into underground or stone hiding places. But she had seen tracks of mammalian life—huge tracks. These worried her most. Bears, mountain lions? They had slept in a cave once occupied by a black bear, so she knew they lived here. And Minnie had identified a mountain lion's screeching the first night above Copperhead Canyon when Maddie had thought she heard a woman screaming. These were not desert creatures, and she suspected they had ventured from their more natural habitat of the mountains or canyons on travels to prospective hunting grounds.

She kept an eye out for water sources but saw no prospects. Thirst had become a constant for her, but she rationed her water intake carefully, hoping that the black mountain would offer water sources. She could turn south and find the stream she and Minnie had followed, but the odds of encountering Moon or confirming her trail for him would increase considerably.

As the sun eased nearer the horizon, Maddie began to search for a place to rest and catch some sleep if her worries would allow. There was so much to think about. The mountain was her goal, but what then? She could not live there forever. And how would she live at all? Her father would have employed someone to search for her. She had no doubt of that, but how would such persons find her? And there was Moon, possibly others of the so-called Blue Bandana gang tracking her by now.

She tried to judge the distance to the mountains, guessing that perhaps another three hours would take her to the base. She was a mountain girl and knew nature was deceptive when it came to mountain farness. Regardless, she did not intend to make an ascent into the hills after sunset when the night hunters ventured out, and any trails would be more treacherous.

She had about given up the notion of locating a cave or a decent natural shelter when she spotted a group of three or four juniper trees at the top of a rise no more than fifty paces west. She liked the notion of elevation, where she might see someone—or something—approaching. The trees would offer some cover and as much sanctuary as she could hope for this night. Suddenly very tired, she angled toward the trees and found her legs almost giving out as she negotiated the slope. She collapsed on the ground when she reached the junipers, pleased to find a healthy patch of shortgrass to cushion her sleeping place.

She sat beneath the motionless tree branches, savoring the shade they provided, and leaned against the trunk of the largest juniper, which she guessed was more than twenty feet tall, twice the height of the three trees clustered randomly about like children accompanying their mother on an outing. Maddie surveyed the desolate land around her, half expecting Minnie to come racing over the horizon. Again, she pledged that her friend would walk through the world beside her, that she would keep Minnie alive through her own life's journey. She could see a considerable distance from this spot and saw no sign of Moon or any other life, save for a few vultures swooping above her, checking her out as a prospective meal, she supposed.

She permitted herself a few swigs from the canteen, still saving enough for a few drinks the next morning, knowing she was barely drinking enough to sustain her. She was drowsy now and got to her knees and spread out the robe. A nap would be nice. Ordinarily, she would pee first, but that well was dry. She knew that was not a good sign. If she did not find water, tomorrow could bring the end. Right now, though, her only thought was sleep. She curled up in a fetal position on the robe and closed her eyes. In a few minutes, all worries were swept away.

It was dark when she awakened hours later, but a half moon and star-spangled sky cast a lamp-like glow over the prairie that rescued her from a pitch-black blindness. She was chilly now and tugged the robe about her body before propping herself up on one elbow and looking out over the dusky landscape. She loved the quiet of this lonely land, wondered what it would be like to live in this place. Always. Maybe Minnie would find peace here.

She tensed when she saw movement behind some mesquite shrubs to the northeast. She did not want to reveal her location but grasped her Winchester, which she had leaned against the trunk of the big tree and pulled it into the robe. Her eyes fixed on the bushes, she watched and waited until finally something crept out from behind the mesquite. It was not a man, but her sigh of relief was cut short when a huge creature emerged, nose to the ground.

It was a shadowy mass. It lifted its head high, probably trying to pick up a scent. Wolf? Mountain lion? She did not think it was a bear. It was moving her way now. She tightened her grip on the rifle, pondering whether to cast off the robe and position to shoot. Maddie was certain she could not deliver a kill shot in the darkness and would likely only enrage the beast, so she thought better of it. Play dead, she decided. And do not run. Old Ben, her father's ranch foreman had told her once that running was an invitation for a mountain lion to give chase. Few would otherwise attack a human unless cornered. She burrowed into the buffalo robe, pulling it over her head, clutching its edges tightly as she rolled over onto her belly and froze.

When it arrived, she felt a paw scratching at the robe and a nose probing here and there. She heard the creature breathing and sniffing, sensed it circling her cocoon. She started to pray silently to the God she had discarded when her devout father departed the family home, leaving her behind. Then she felt the beast pressing the robe against her flesh. She could swear it was lying down beside her, evidently deciding to nap against the softness of the old robe. Yes, the visitor was motionless now, but she could hear its breathing and an occasional snort. She was trapped. And suddenly she had to pee, the pressure feeling like every drop of water that had passed her lips yesterday had traveled directly to her bladder. She tried not to think about her urgency, but then that was all she could think about, almost forgetting about her sleeping companion.

She had almost resigned herself to wetting her britches when the creature moved again, apparently getting to its feet. And then it whined and pawed again at the robe, near her shoulder. She didn't think big cats whined. She supposed wolves or coyotes might but not likely at their prey. She tugged back the top of the robe, inched her head out and squinted against the first rays of sunrise before being greeted by a pair of yellow eyes, and then a wet tongue slapped across her forehead. A dog. The biggest dog she had ever seen. She tossed the robe aside and sat up, looking at the animal in disbelief, instinctively wiping her arm across her face as it continued its moist welcome with tail wagging happily.

She hugged the dog's neck briefly but had other business more urgent. She jumped up and hurried down the slope to flatter ground, dropped her britches, squatted and emptied her bladder's contents with relief. The dog watched from afar, but, gratefully, had given her space. Finished, she returned to the buffalo robe and waiting canine.

She examined the dog more closely now. Decidedly male. Short hair, erect ears but a strange calico coloring of blue-black, orange and white splotches with the black descending over one eye like a pirate's patch. She decided that she would call him "Pirate" if he stuck around. She wondered if he was part wolf. She loved dogs and, before she had gotten obsessed with Wally, had read a fair amount about the different breeds. Her visitor's coloring might fit some of the Australian dogs she had read about. But the size did not fit. And the eyes. She had seen wolves with eyes like these.

Pirate's hide revealed signs of battles past, scabbed wounds on his muzzle and under his jaw and deep claw marks raked across one shoulder, healing now but looking as if they might have festered earlier.

But what was he doing here? Was there an owner nearby? And would he be friend or enemy? She was confident the dog had not accompanied Moon. Minnie would have said something if a dog had been with the pursuers.

She had nothing to feed the dog—or herself—but he did not seem to be starving. He was a rangy animal but appeared strong and energetic, just looking for a companion, it seemed. A dog like this could likely scare up his own meals without much trouble. She welcomed him and hoped he would stay, but it would be his choice.

Chapter 30

I T WAS EARLY, but she had no camp chores, so she rolled up the buffalo robe and gathered up her rifle and bag. Fixing her eyes on the skunk stripe that ran down the black mountain wall, she renewed her journey to the mountain. Pirate fell in beside her.

Her new friend brightened her mood, lessened the feeling of aloneness and noticeably reduced her fear, although she had no illusions that Pirate would become her protector. As the morning wore on, she found herself talking to the dog and easily fell into creating his responses.

"How far to the mountains, Pirate? An hour or two, you say?"

"Yes, that looks about right. We're gaining ground. I think we'll be at the base mid-morning. Will there be water? There will be? I agree. I've never seen a mountain without water."

Pirate looked up at her whenever she spoke and did not seem to mind the sound of her voice. Each time he lifted his head toward her, he offered silent reassurance. As they neared the base of the black mountain, she saw that the skunk stripe she had sighted was a discoloration in a sheer wall of stone that she estimated reached over two hundred feet above the base. Scaling this obstacle would have been hopeless, but she noticed that the mountain tapered off to the east and that the escarpment gave way to less steep rock.

Most important, though, was the discovery of water, lots of it. A river lined with willows, cottonwoods and even a few oaks and generous stretches of short grass along its south bank. At this segment, the north side of the river edged the mountain wall. She questioned now whether the formation, which seemed endless going west, earned the rank of mountain by her standards, which had been established by the snow-capped peaks of the Rockies that towered above her family's ranch valley. She gazed upward. There were no peaks here, and the surface seemed to flatten off into a plateau or mesa in the high rocks.

"Well, Pirate, I'm needing water, but I don't want to boil it here. I'd feel safer after we cross to the other side."

She began walking easterly along the bank, seeking a potential crossing. She was a good swimmer. Tom Sanford bragged that his daughter could swim like an otter, and she did not worry about her personal safety in making the crossing, but she needed to keep her Winchester, ammunition and lucifers dry. The river was not running high and was clear above the reddish riverbed. Pirate raced out ahead, and at first she thought he was abandoning her, but he stopped abruptly and waited at the water's edge, looking at her expectantly. Was he trying to tell her something?

She stopped and cast her eyes over the opposite side of the river. It was wider here and the water slow-moving. There was a flat area on the north bank, and she thought she saw traces of a deer trail leading up the mesa's face. Why not? She slipped out of her moccasins, then her britches and stuffed them in the bag. Her shirt did not quite cover her bare butt, but she didn't think Pirate cared. She stepped into the water, welcoming its coolness. The footing was soft, yet solid beneath the loose clay and dirt. With each step a red swirl rose and clouded the water, but the river never flowed above her thighs. Pirate half walked and half swam behind her. When they stepped out onto the sandbar that formed the bank at this juncture, Pirate showered her some as he shook the water free of his coat, but she figured he had earned that right. She got dressed again and looked around.

She saw Pirate lapping water from a little pool along a trail not more than a dozen paces up a path leading from the sandbar into the black mesa rock, which she noted had the same strange texture of the stone that marked Minnie's grave. The water seemed to be flowing over the path and dropping as a miniature waterfall into a streambed that snaked its way to the river. She joined the dog and saw that the water was erupting like a little geyser from a fissure in the black-gray rock wall and emptying into the pool that overflowed and sent the water on. An underground spring. She bent over and touched a finger to the water in the pool. Ice cold. No wonder Pirate headed up this way. He obviously knew the territory. The water from the wall should be as pure as good well water. She filled her canteen from the natural fountain and drank till she felt sick before refilling it.

Pirate had started up the trail and waited for her at a turn. The dog seemed in a hurry, so she decided to accommodate him. She was ready for a rest, though, and would demand a break higher up. She could not explain why, but she knew she would feel safer at the summit of this mountain or mesa. High ground. That was what she liked. She wondered how many entrances there were to this plateau, which she assumed continued for a considerable distance, perhaps many miles. She wondered if she should lie in wait for Moon at the top of the trail and ambush him when he came up. But he might never show. He might have already abandoned the chase, and she questioned whether he would bother to take on the mesa climb if he reached the river.

Maddie stopped along the trail several times during the trek to the top of the mesa. The slope was gradual but constant, twisting between crevices in the unusual black and sometimes porous-looking rock. Along the outer edge, the trail was wide and footing stable, not intimidating or frightening to her. Mostly, it felt to her as if she were climbing into the bowels of a stone fortress. It was mid-afternoon when she found herself at the mesa's top. She sat down on a flat-topped boulder to catch her breath again. She cast her eyes about the mesa. Not quite as level as a table, but mostly terrain that would be described as flat except for occasional stone upheavals and scatterings of rocks, large and small. More grass and trees than she had expected. To the west and north, she could see no end to the plateau. She remained near the south border, however, and she could see where it dropped off to the east.

Pirate barked impatiently. He had taken to bossing quite naturally, it seemed, but he seemed to have a destination in mind. She could follow him for a spell yet and look for a place to set up a camp of sorts along the way. No more than a half hour later, she stopped abruptly. Impossible. A gray, stone cabin backed by a small forest of juniper and cedar on the north and west. She slowly walked toward the structure, circling to the south where the entrance seemed to be, noticing now a log lean-to set back twenty paces from the cabin, large enough for two or three horses and some hay storage at most. A sturdy outhouse sat between the house and lean-to.

She swung around in front of the cabin. The door was wide open, and a gunnysack covering the sole window fluttered in the wind. Pirate trotted into the house, looked back at her and gave her a few quick barks. What was this all about? She dropped the rolled robe and bag on the ground but held onto her Winchester. She stepped cautiously through the doorway, attracted immediately by the beautiful fireplace constructed of a mix of gray and white stones interspersed with the shining ebony rocks that covered so much of the landscape. The cabin was floored with flat stones as well. The single room was austerely furnished. Off to her right, she saw a single chair and a table topped with split logs. Rows of shelves with cooking implements, even some supplies. Her eyes fastened on cans of fruit and beans, and immediately she realized how famished she was.

She looked to the right where Pirate sat now beside a bed pushed up against the west wall. She stepped in that direction but stopped when she saw the skull with its not quite toothless mouth grinning up at her from the bed. A few weeks earlier she might have turned away and vomited. But she was a seasoned killer now and had buried her best friend. She stepped tentatively closer, reaching out and pulling back the gunnysack to allow more light through the window.

The bones were stripped clean, scattered about the bedcover, a few on the floor. A musty odor permeated the single room, but it was not a repulsive smell. She knew little about such things but guessed that the man must have died at least several months ago, and nature's cleanup squad must have entered the cabin to take care of the remains. The healing wounds on Pirate's back were possibly incurred while he guarded his master's body for some time after the man's death. She released the burlap curtain, her eyes accustomed to the dusky interior now, and stepped closer to the bed. Pirate looked up at her expectantly and wagged his tail. She patted his head and scratched his ears, and he responded with a soft chortle.

"Well, fella, I'm sorry. This man must've been your friend. I suppose the two of you lived here together. I don't think you're more than a few years old. I'll bet he raised you from a pup. We'll give him a decent burial. Maybe that'll give you some peace."

She took one end of the blanket and began to shake the bones toward the middle, and then did the same with the other. She picked up the loose bones on the floor and added them to the pile. She thought she was missing a lower leg bone and an upper arm bone, but she wasn't certain and was not about to take on the puzzle of putting the skeleton together. When she had the bones and skull in a heap, she pulled the ends and sides of the blanket cover together and carried what remained of the nameless man outside.

She walked to the lean-to and was surprised to find an assortment of tools at one end, including shovels, pickaxes, hammers and saws. There were several wheelbarrows and a stack of buckets. She wondered if the man had been a miner searching for, perhaps finding, gold or silver here. She selected a likely spade and paced the area in the vicinity of the cabin seeking a burial site, Pirate following her patiently. She found what she was looking for not more than twenty feet northeast of the cabin, a cemetery cleared of stones and brush and fenced off with posts and timbers.

She stepped through the narrow opening and examined the three markers in the plot, which she estimated at about fifteen feet by fifteen feet. Three slabs of cedar, the ends of which seemed firmly buried. Carved on the front of one was "KING 1872." The others read "WOLF 1880" and "LUCY 1881." She assumed the occupants were dogs, especially King and Wolf. Perhaps, Wolf and Lucy were Pirate's parents. On the other hand, Lucy could have been the man's wife or daughter. But wouldn't he have entered birthdates, possibly last names? Maybe there was something in the house that would unlock the mysteries.

She began digging a grave next to Lucy's. It was easy digging for two feet and then she hit solid rock. She lowered the blanket wrapped bones into the shallow grave and filled it up. She rolled a large stone to the head of the grave, placing it near Lucy's marker. That was the best she could do for now. She stood back and gazed at the somber scene. It was so peaceful here. Minnie would like it. She wondered if she could someday return and locate Minnie's bones and bury them here, where she would not be alone. On second thought, she decided, she wanted Minnie's remains buried near her own last resting place. With that thought, she turned away and headed to the cabin to see if there was salvageable food in the cans that were shelved there. Pirate walked beside her.

Chapter 31

THE CIMARRON RIVER channel had been napping when Trace and Darby crossed it this time. They had remained astride their mounts without so much as wetting the toes of their boots when the buckskin and blood bay waded through the river that had nearly claimed their lives with flooding, raging waters nearly three months earlier. This afternoon, the Beaver River appeared no more threatening, but if they had not been misled, there was no need to cross to the south bank of the Beaver. Less than a few hours' journey along the north bank should lead them to a sharp bend south in the river's course. At that place, they were to depart the river for a spell, ride due west until they met the Beaver on its journey back north. The northernmost point of the Beaver's path should place them within an hour's ride northwesterly to the Copperhead Canyon hideout.

The riders dismounted near the riverbank to rest and water the horses. Trace stretched, and then began pacing back and forth, rubbing his lower back while he walked. His rear was feeling the saddle time, too.

Darby remarked, "You haven't done any serious riding for a spell. You're paying for it."

"I haven't seen you on a horse that much lately, either."

"I've got more padding on my butt."

"I never noticed. Show me."

She stuck her tongue out at him. "You good for a few more hours? We've got at least that till sundown. But we can stop anytime you want if you're too sore and tired."

She was goading him now. But it worked. There was no way he would call it a day after those words. "I can ride all night if you want."

"That won't be necessary. The horses will need a break by then. It will be a cold camp again. No coffee, and we're down to the dried biscuits and jerky."

Coffee. He would pass up the biscuits and jerky for a cup of hot coffee given a choice. He pulled the Timex watch from his pocket. "Ten past three. Yeah, let's move on. Horses are holding up fine. We'll stop about six and have time to stake out the horses and get them settled in before dark. We'll want to be on our way again by sunrise tomorrow."

Darby asked, "How far do you think we've got from the Beaver's south turn to where we pick it up again?"

"Don't know about distance, but Jim-Bob thought it might be a short day's ride. If he's right, we could hit there later tomorrow afternoon."

"And then what?"

"If Copperhead Canyon is only an hour from there, we might take a romantic moonlight ride up that way," Trace said.

"I won't count on the romance part, but I'm anxious to get there. I'm worried that we're going to end up coming a long way for nothing. I hadn't planned on paying to bury seven outlaws. The expense of lodging and feeding everybody in Denver. Salary for Clay and now that bounty hunter or whatever he is."

"It's only money." Trace steeled himself for a scolding that never came.

Instead, Darby swung into the saddle and nudged Cinnamon into a steady lope west, following the river. When he caught up, he reined the buckskin in close to her, and they rode silently side by side for a spell.

Finally, he broke the silence. "Are you pissed at me?"

She turned her head and looked at him, only the mischievous glint in her dark brown eyes betraying an otherwise solemn face. "No, but you were baiting me. I decided not to bite."

"Me? Why would you think that?"

"You're always saying I worry too much about money."

"And you're always saying I don't worry enough about it."

"If you ever want to see your own cattle on that tall-grass prairie we own, maybe you should worry a little more about money."

"You worry enough for both of us, Love," Trace replied, "but the next few days, I'll try to help ease your worries some." He blew her a kiss and nudged Atlas ahead, knowing that things would be fine between them next stop.

As anticipated, a few hours later the Beaver River started its sharp turn south, where a map they had studied for their previous trip to No Man's Land indicated it would make a brief visit to the Texas panhandle before hooking back north again. The barren landscape offered few decent campsites, but near the river, a few cottonwoods thrived, and grass for grazing was adequate. They unsaddled the horses and led them to water before staking them in the grass nearby. Darby rationed out the biscuits and jerky, holding back enough for two more skimpy meals.

"We're going to be down to roots and berries tomorrow night," she observed.

"I haven't seen a berry anyplace."

"Neither have I. I guess that leaves roots."

"Darned few of those around here. I'm not sure junipers and cedars are edible. Still some grasshoppers and beetles around. I ate some of those once when I had a patrol under siege by Comanches in the Palo Duro Canyon for two weeks. Never acquired a taste for the things, though."

"I'm a long way from being that hungry."

Night had fully cast its dark blanket over No Man's Land by the time they finished their meager meal, and they laid out their bedrolls, forming a large shared double as had become their habit. They peeled off their boots and burrowed into the blankets. Darby spooned up next to Trace, tossing her arm over his midsection, and they raced each other to sleep, Trace vaguely aware that Darby had narrowly won the competition, before he dropped off.

It was late afternoon the next day when they sighted the Beaver River again snaking its course northwesterly. They reined their horses toward the nearside bank and followed the river upstream until the channel made a gradual turn southwesterly.

Trace said, "This must be the place Jim-Bob spoke of. All we know is that the canyon should be an hour or so northwest. No landmarks except a stream that runs through it and leaves the canyon and turns south."

"Couldn't we keep going west and find a stream and follow it north? It probably eventually ends up in the Beaver River. Creeks and streams are few and far between out here. Odds are we wouldn't find the wrong one. There aren't that many."

"Yeah, I think we go more west than north for a spell. You never know about streams in this part of the country. When I rode with Mackenzie during the Comanche wars, we'd find streams and think we were going to follow them, and then, all at once, they'd flow into some rocks and disappear, head underground, maybe for miles before they'd surface again. No Man's Land reminds me a lot of parts of west Texas. Anyway, if you're game, we'll keep going. I'd really like to hole up not far from the canyon tonight. Find a place on the rim where we can use the spyglass."

"I'm more than game. The two Bandanas that got away should have been back for a day now. I'm worried that the outfit's going to disappear with the gold and the girl."

Chapter 32

BAXTER CORKER AND Goose Carver had returned to the canyon that morning, but Corker, by nature a calm and deliberate man, had been on the edge of outright panic ever since. Of his usual crew, all that remained were Goose, Gimpy Smith, who had stayed behind this job, and himself. He didn't include the Comanch, Moon Parker, and Bull Killer and Smoke Brown, who had been out tracking the Sanford kid and the mulatto whore for more than three days now. They were on their own, and he did not want any part of anything that happened with the girl. There was no question she would have to die because she could identify too many members of the Blue Bandana Gang.

By his count, there were seven men from the other crew left in the canyon, including their crew leader, Arlo Shales, a feisty, surly man who was not about to cede any authority to a failed crew leader. Shales had been outraged when he learned that three of his own crew loaned to Corker had been taken down during the bumbled heist.

Corker's sense was that the canyon should be abandoned as soon as possible. It was likely someone in his crew had been taken alive. Assuming that was the case, sooner or later, a captive would be spitting out the hideout's location in a deal to save his own hide. He had heard of an old saying about "honor among thieves." He had lived among thieves for over twenty-five years and long ago concluded that was pure fable. He had not met a thief yet who wouldn't sell out a comrade to save his own neck. He did not exclude himself. He, Goose and Gimpy had been making plans to help themselves to as much of the gold bullion as they could stuff into their saddlebags and ride out tomorrow. That would necessitate killing a guard posted at the overseer's cabin, where the gold was being held.

His plan was shot to hell when the overseer, Bart Wince, returned about suppertime and called the two crew leaders to his cabin to talk. They sat at the eating table in the single-room cabin, a crudely built log structure no better than those occupied by other gang members. Of course, Wince resided elsewhere most of the time and only appeared in the canyon to deliver instructions or transport the stolen bounty to the big boss's custody. On those occasions, he was invariably accompanied by two or three guards. Tonight, Wince was unaccompanied.

Corker dreaded telling Wince about the failed train robbery. He wondered if the overseer had already been informed by Corker's rival, Shales, or Gramps McBride, a "swing man," who rode with whichever crew required a team and wagon. Corker also suspected Gramps of being placed with the gang as something of a spy for Wince. The old man never had much to say, but Wince always seemed to know what had taken place during his absence, and Corker had seen Gramps entering and leaving Wince's cabin on several occasions following the overseer's return to Copperhead Canyon.

Wince poured each of the crew leaders a steaming cup of coffee before filling his own tin cup. "Things are serious, boys. Time to close shop."

"You know what happened up in Kansas then?" Corker asked.

Wince, a bronze-skinned man with black hair combed straight back, looked at Corker with cold, obsidian eyes. Corker was sure Indian blood ran in his veins. "I got a telegram from Denver, and I rode right back. Brought along a spare horse so I could keep going. I got some of the details when I came in before I called you two up here. I heard you lost seven, maybe eight, men."

Corker hated admitting this again, especially with the beady-eyed Shales sitting there as smug as a pig pissing. "Yeah, I did. They was ready for us. We was set up for this. Pinkertons."

"Were any of the men left behind still alive?"

Corker shrugged. "I can't say for sure. They had us outnumbered, gunfire coming from everyplace. We had to beat the hell out."

"I was told the Sanford girl and Smoke's and Bull's whore escaped, too. Those two and Moon were supposed to be chasing them down."

"You know as much about that as I do. We were on our way to the job when that happened. Shales and I traded some men because one of mine was wounded on the last job, the Comanch kid couldn't be trusted, and the other two was lodged near the girl and keeping an eye on her. Them and Gimp."

"The Comanch kid is my nephew. Doesn't look like those men kept a very good eye out. Even let their whore get loose."

He should have kept his mouth shut about Comanch. He had always wondered if the uncontrollable kid might have a family connection to Wince. Well, he was about done with this outfit anyhow. He just wanted to grab some money and ride as far away from this place as he could get.

Shales spoke. "You said it's time to close shop. You ain't calling the Blue Bandanas quits are you?"

"That's the order from the top. We're pulling out. Tomorrow morning, the gold gets loaded in Gramp's buckboard. I've got more than enough cash to pay the men, especially since we've got less men than I figured on. I'll have bonuses for five men who go with me as guards to the delivery point. You two got first chance, but it doesn't matter. I want five men who can follow orders and use a gun."

"Whoa, just a minute," Shales said. "What about the extra money the other boys would've took if they hadn't got themselves shot?"

"That's none of your concern. You'll all get the share you're entitled to."

"But somebody else is getting more than their share— either you or the big boss . . . the general some calls him."

Corker had wondered about that but had been reluctant to cause a fuss. He wanted out, and he wasn't interested in being a guard. He had a bad feeling that the dominoes had started to fall. He had squirreled away most of his share from other jobs, and with his cut of the big gold haul, his working days were done. Find a woman and settle down someplace. Maybe a little ranch and a few cows. But he did think the survivors ought to share the amount due the dead men. He decided to back Shales up on that matter.

Corker said, "I agree with Shales. That money ought to be split by those of us that are left." He could see Wince's angry eyes smoldering. The overseer was likely planning to claim that share for himself.

"You greedy bastards. That wasn't a part of the bargain."

Corker, feeling braver now that Wince was cornered, pressed, "Tell us you weren't taking that share for yourself. Course, we wouldn't believe you nohow."

Shales joined in. "Consider this: what if we was just to take that gold for ourselves? You're outnumbered. Hell, you couldn't stop us."

Wince had an answer to that, one Corker hadn't thought of when he was planning to make off with some of the gold. The overseer, more confident now, said, "And what are you going to do with two-pound bricks of gold? You can't take them to a bank to trade for cash. Local sheriff or marshal will be there before you get out the door. It wouldn't take a minute to tie you to the Blue Bandanas. In a week or two, you'd have the noose squeezing about your neck. That gold is worthless to you if you don't know how to market it."

Neither Shales nor Corker had a comeback. Coins were one thing. Uncoined bullion was another.

Wince said, "I'll hold back the shares for Smoke, Bull and Moon. If we leave before they get back, Moon knows where to find me. You can divide the shares of the dead men amongst the men that are here. And I'll pay five hundred each to the men that come with me to guard the gold."

"I'll buy into that," Shales said. "But I want to know just how much time's going to be wrapped up in the guard detail. How far we going?"

"I guess it won't hurt to say now. Trinidad, Colorado. Two days almost straight west by horseback with a spare mount. Could be twice that by wagon. There's some rugged country between here and there. No real wagon trail except a short spell on the old Cimarron cut-off before heading due west."

"I don't want no part of the guard business," Corker said. "I'll help load and see you off, but then I'm done."

"For a thousand," Shales said, "I'll go with you and line up the right men."

Wince was silent for a bit, rubbing his chin thoughtfully. "You've got a deal. Tell your men that payday will be in the morning after the wagon is loaded and ready to move out. If they got stuff in the canyon they don't want to leave behind, they'd better start packing."

Chapter 33

C LAY SIBLEY TUGGED gently at the pack mule's lead rope as he nudged his bay gelding southwest along the ruts of what Colmes had said was the Cimarron cut-off of the Santa Fe Trail. The trail, once a major corridor for commerce and migration to the west, was being quickly relegated to the past by railroad tracks spreading out like a giant spider web over the land. The iron horse was changing the country.

Colmes claimed to have scouted the area for the Army and Custer's Seventh U. S. Cavalry during the fall and winter of 1868, almost fourteen years earlier. Clay had learned this when the man had started speaking again a day out of Garden City. His scouting had taken him into the Indian Territory further east on the Washita River, where he and Osage scouts had located Black Kettle's Southern Cheyenne village. Black Kettle had thought he was at peace with the whites when his village was attacked that late November day and countless women and children slaughtered with the unsuspecting warriors. Black Kettle and his wife, Medicine Woman, died that day as well.

The Washita Massacre vaulted Custer to the top of the list of white soldiers feared and hated by the tribes that would finally exact revenge at the Little Big Horn in June of 1876. Even Ted Colmes, who appeared to have a strong stomach for violence, said he had been sickened with what happened on the Washita River and had terminated his scouting tour when his contract expired.

Clay called to Audra, who was astride her Appaloosa on the opposite side of the wagon ruts. "Water the horses? There's a stream that feeds into the Cimarron off to your left."

She waved acknowledgment and nodded her head in agreement, reining her mount off onto a deer trail that angled toward the stream flowing toward the river, perhaps fifty yards distant. They dismounted and led the animals to the stream bank to drink. It was mid-afternoon, and Clay figured they would ride till dusk. The sky was mostly overcast with a wink of blue peering from time to time between billowing clouds. A breeze made the day a pleasant one for beast and rider. No sign of a serious storm ahead. It should be safe to build a fire tonight, and they had added to provisions at Ulysses, an outpost on the prairie that the storekeeper said was not yet a legal town but would be soon. They had made the town in a day's ride from Garden City and camped the previous night a few miles south along the Cimarron.

Audra said, "What do you think Colmes is up to?"

"I'm taking him at his word. He's looking for Copperhead Canyon. It's a one-man job. We can't risk being seen. We've got to surprise them. We can't overwhelm by numbers."

"He said we might not see him till tomorrow and not to be concerned if another night went by. It makes me uneasy."

"I think he's embarrassed about what happened in Garden City. He loosened up a little last night when he told me about his scouting experiences and the Washita Massacre, but he's avoiding you like the plague. He was glad for the excuse to get out on his own."

"But I haven't treated him any differently. Heck, I'm not even mad at him. You heard what he said about me last night. By the way, I didn't swallow that little fib you told for a second, mister. You did hear. And it was the truth. I don't remember him from those times, but I can see how he might have thought—especially in his drunken state—that I was available. That's not an excuse for his behavior. But I can forgive it. I've done plenty in my time that needs forgiving. What's done is done."

"That's part of what's bothering him, I suspect."

"What do you mean?"

"My uncle, Charley Nighthorse, told me once, 'Forgive your enemies; it messes up their heads.' Well, I don't think Ted's your enemy, but the granting of true forgiveness is not a common thing in my experience. Only the kind and wise can do it. But when it happens, it often befuddles the recipient and leaves them with something else to come to terms with."

"You're quite a philosopher for a man who hardly ever talks. Of course, you're an educated man. Even graduated college, I'd say."

His gelding had finished drinking and tossed its head, showing interest in some grass a few paces away. Clay led the horse and mule to a patch of grass. "They've earned a snack," he said.

Audra followed him with her mare. "Well, tell me I'm wrong."

"How do you guess these things?"

"No guess. I've had my own education, you might say."

"Oberlin College. Ohio. Law."

"Law? You're a lawyer?"

"Not technically. I've never taken the bar examination anyplace. Allan Pinkerton came to the school while I was in my final year. He was looking for Negro agents, and Oberlin had been recruiting black students and offering scholarship benefits since the 1830s. The work, especially the undercover part, fascinated me, and I wasn't aware of many places where I might make a living as a lawyer. I grabbed the job, but after I was there a few years, Mister Pinkerton said Army experience would be beneficial if I wanted to grow my opportunities with the agency. That's how I ended up with the buffalo soldiers. Good as his word, Mister Pinkerton had a job for me when my enlistment was up. If I'd known the risks I was signing on for with the Army, I'd have passed on that phase of my education."

"I'm impressed, a little intimidated."

"Not intimidated. I don't think you know the meaning of the word. Now we'd better ride."

As they continued their journey along the edges of the cut-off trail, Clay glanced over at the pixie-like woman who sat erect and alert in her saddle. He swore he had never seen such a beautiful creature, but it was the spirit and intellect beneath that veneer that attracted him. Regardless, he had to resist the pull. The last time he had acted upon such feelings had put a noose about his neck.

Chapter 34

AUDRA AND CLAY tore down and rolled their pup tents, delayed by a heavy dew that had left the tent canvas damp and a morning sun that promised to dry the tents if they allowed a bit of time. To pack the tents wet would have invited mold and seam rot. They would have broken camp anyway, but they had the luxury of a more leisurely pace this morning. Ted Colmes had instructed the detectives to stay with the Cimarron River. If he did not intercept them before they reached the place he called the black mesa, they were to set up camp near the river at the base of the mesa, and he would find them there.

Audra had savored a few extra hours sleep this morning since she and Clay had agreed there was no reason to be in the saddle before the birds woke this day. And then she had awakened to the aroma of coffee, biscuits and bacon drifting into the tent. Clay had seen to getting the fire started and tending to all the breakfast chores, and when she crawled out of the tent, had teased, "Sorry. No breakfast in bed this morning."

"Your spoiling me," she had said. "I should have been up."

"Lady needs a little spoiling once in a while. Better come eat while everything's fresh and hot."

It had been a pleasant breakfast. The food and companionship. She liked Clay Sibley and felt they were becoming fast friends. He was still an enigma to her, this educated mixed-blood man, who had found his place with the Pinkerton National Detective Agency, even fought Comanches to enhance his opportunities there. She wanted to learn more about him, but she knew it would be like pulling teeth to get him to disclose much. She would have to settle for a morsel at a time. In the meantime, she was enjoying her time alone with Clay, comfortable with the long silences that passed between them.

After they finished hitching the gear on the pack mule, Audra got out the map she had sketched, opened it and passed the paper to Clay. "Do you have any idea where we're at on this? I know we're on the Cimarron River, but this isn't drawn to scale. I've got the black mesa at the west end of No Man's Land, but that could be three days' ride for all I know."

"I think we're about here." He moved closer to her, held up the map and pointed at a spot on the sketched river line. "From what Colmes said, I'm betting we get there about high noon if we don't laze around the rest of the morning. He said we'd get sight of it about an hour away."

Clay folded the map and handed it back, and her acute awareness when their fingers touched distracted her for just a moment. She stepped back and moved toward her saddled mare.

"What if Colmes doesn't show up by tomorrow morning?" Audra asked.

"We can't wait forever. I don't guess we'd have much choice. We would have to take up our own hunt for the canyon. We can't leave Trace and Darby on their own without our trying to find them. Hopefully, he'll be back and tell us that he's found the canyon and talked with Trace and Darby, too."

Chapter 35

AFTER MADDIE SANFORD buried the remains of the apparent cabin owner, Pirate, her new friend and companion, seemed to calm. She re-entered the cabin to attend to her first priority—food. Rummaging through the cupboards and shelves, she found that mesa wildlife occupants, probably raccoons in the forefront, had already raided the place, tearing open any bagged staples and removing the lids of storage tins, to dump the contents on the floor. Mounds of flour and coffee on the floor remained, but most of the sugar granules had been licked up.

She found enough dented but unopened cans of beans, peaches and apples on the floor, however, to constitute a banquet for someone in her starved condition. And there seemed to be an ample store of salvageable cans to provide food for many days, if necessary. She found a big screwdriver in the cupboard with assorted forks, knives and spoons and used it to punch holes in the can tops and pry them open sufficiently to empty the contents. Although she had run across some tin plates and cups, she retrieved a spoon and made a feast of beans and peaches directly from the cans, saving half of each for her next meal.

Maddie realized she had eaten too much, too fast, when her stomach rebelled and threatened to toss back the contents, but she stepped outside and sat down on a stump that had been placed in front of the dwelling for apparently that purpose. Pirate pressed his nose under her arm for attention, and she scratched her friend's ears and stroked his head, while they both basked in the sun's rays and enjoyed a gentle breeze. She loved the peace here and wondered about the man who had apparently built the cabin and eked out a lonely life in this place. She supposed her questions would never be answered, but even in death he had granted her refuge and sent a warrior to guide and protect her. She was not alone, and she was so grateful for that.

But now what? She could not remain here forever. On the other hand, a wrangler at the ranch told her once that if she ever got lost in the mountains above the ranch valley to just stay put. Don't try to find somebody. Let the searchers find you. Since she had no idea where to go from here, it seemed like good advice. She knew her father would have folks looking for her by now, perhaps an army of people. The only flaw in her plan she could see was that Moon might also be looking. Still, here she could prepare and fortify for an attack. Also, after enough time had passed, she could build a fire in the fireplace. Hopefully, the right person would see smoke and come to investigate. Regardless, she was tired of running.

After her stomach settled, Maddie got up and went to work, always keeping her rifle within reach and her eyes on the surrounding plateau. Fortunately, the flat lay of the land and a landscape with little undergrowth enhanced her view. She located the water source within a hundred feet of the cabin, a rippling, clear stream that cut through the stone from the west and seemed to be headed for the Cimarron River edging the base of the mesa. She scavenged two buckets from the lean-to and filled them from the stream and carried the water to the cabin.

The broom in a corner of the cabin had been swept nearly to a stub, but she cleaned the house as best she could, flinching when she caught sight of bone slivers and chips in the dust pile. She decided to use the bed, and, after removing the smelly and filthy bedding, she installed her buffalo robe on the dirty straw mattress, deciding she preferred familiar stink to the odors left behind by a man's corpse.

The sack-covered window had shutters that could be closed and latched top, center and bottom from inside, and the thick oak door was imbedded with a large deadbolt lock. She figured that the narrow openings between the stones on each side of the door must be gun slots. The structure had obviously been designed with defense in mind. This made sense since the cabin had doubtless been there a spell, and not many years back Indians were likely frequent visitors. Perhaps the builder had been a trader who enjoyed immunity from attack or was at least tolerated by the tribes. Otherwise, it seemed unlikely that even his little fortress could have withstood a large-scale assault.

She could not find an oil lamp or even a candle in the cabin, and she debated building a fire in the fireplace just for some light as the sun began its crawl down the western horizon. There was a small stack of wood next to the house, and she still had some lucifers in her bag. She finally abandoned the notion, worrying that the smell of smoke, if not the sight of it, might signal Moon of her presence on the mesa.

She sat down at the table and ate the remainder of the beans and peaches, and then went outside to visit the privy, which she found luxurious in comparison to the primitive facilities at Copperhead Canyon. She returned to the cabin, followed by Pirate, who had stood watch while she did her business at the outhouse. Joined by the dog, she went back into the house, closed and locked the shutters and the door and was momentarily blinded by the cave-like darkness. She felt her way to the bed and sat down on the mattress, trying to erase from her mind that a man had died there. As her eyes adjusted to the darkness, she felt more comfortable with her abode. Slivers of moonlight sneaked between the shutters and the gun slots, allowing her to more easily find her way about the room if she needed.

She reached down to assure herself the Winchester was on the floor within easy reach, swung her legs upon the bed and stretched out atop her robe. She pulled the robe about her, not for warmth but for the sense of security it gave her. She started when she felt the bed give and creak and felt the weight settle in beside her. Pirate. *Jumping jehosaphats.* The dog probably weighed as much she did. They were a close fit in the bed, but no way would she boot him out. She slipped her hand out from under the robe and rested it on the dog's shoulder. Her eyes closed, and she dropped into a deep slumber.

Chapter 36

PIRATE'S GROWLING WOKE Maddie the next morning. She had slept so soundly, she had not felt him leave the bed and head for the door, which he sat in front of now. She got up, slipped into her moccasins and with trembling fingers snatched up the Winchester. She must have slept until well into the morning, she thought, seeing bright streams of light sifting through the shutter cracks. Maddie moved quietly to Pirate's side and knelt beside him, wrapping her arm about his neck.

She whispered, "What is it, boy? What's out there?"

Someone rapped tentatively on the door, and she leaped to her feet, stepping away from the door but remaining silent.

"Anybody home?"

She recognized Moon Parker's voice. Pirate commenced growling again. She levered a cartridge into the Winchester's chamber.

The door handle rattled now. "Hey. I know you're in there, Maddie," Parker yelled. "I tracked you here. Found your footprints along the river. Ain't got time to waste. Now you just open up that door, and we'll have us a little chat. Come to terms, as they say. Maybe I won't take you back to the canyon. Your life ain't worth a nickel there. We can go off together someplace if you want. Just the two of us. I won't let nothing happen to you. Maddie, you hear me? You hear me, girl?"

Maddie was paralyzed with indecision. She was temporarily protected in the cabin, but at the same time she was trapped there. Parker began kicking on the door, shaking it on its hinges, but it did not give. Silence. She slipped over to one of the gun slots and peeked through the opening. She saw Parker standing in front of the house, some twenty feet back from the door, his shaggy hair dropping from beneath his hat and onto his shoulders, his hands resting on the pistols holstered on each hip. The crotch and left leg of his faded denims were bloodstained as a result of Minnie's last strike with the knife. She smiled at the thought that Minnie had almost scalped his doodle.

She raised the rifle barrel to the gun slot, but Parker suddenly turned and jogged away in the direction of the lean-to and disappeared from her sight. She had no illusion that he was retreating. She watched and waited for his return. When he appeared again, he was carrying a big axe and headed for the house. She aimed the Winchester but he was a moving target, and her angle was awkward. She squeezed the trigger, and the rifle cracked, the sound echoing off the stone walls and Pirate whining at the sound. She doubted the shot was even close. She readied the rifle to fire again, but by this time, he was out of her line of sight, probably just outside the door, she figured.

Her thought was confirmed when the axe blade dug into the door with a thud. And then another. He was attacking the door with a vengeance, each bite of the axe blade chewing away at the door, shredding it into pieces. Pirate was barking wildly now, and she was forced to push him away, as his front paws scratched at the door, as if wanting to face and take on the invader of their sanctuary.

She could not stop the onslaught on the door, so she must take the axe wielder down when he broke through. If she did not, she knew she was dead. It was only a question of the level of agony that would precede her demise.

She gripped her rifle tightly, realizing only now that Moon Parker's pistols might have the advantage in close quarters fighting.

Suddenly, the tip of the axeblade appeared through the splintered door. She fired the rifle, hoping that lead might pierce the wood and hit the wielder. The reply was another blow, and a follow-up that caved most of the door away. Twice she levered and fired before she saw she was shooting at empty space. Pirate bounded through the ragged doorway, barking and growling fiercely.

Parker screamed and howled in agony. Maddie crawled through the door, still clutching the rifle. Pirate and Parker rolled on the ground in front of the cabin, the dog's jaws clamped on the man's wrist. The arm had already been shredded like meat ripped from a bone. Both Parker and Pirate were covered with blood. The gun that had been held in that hand lay harmlessly a half dozen feet away.

Maddie pointed her rifle at Parker and yelled, "Pirate. No. Stop." To her surprise, the big dog obeyed, released the wrist and backed off, growling threateningly. She almost missed Parker's reach for his other pistol with his still good left hand, but just in time, caught a glimpse of the hand's movement. She squeezed the trigger and drove a bullet into his belly, then for good measure delivered another. Parker moaned, rolled on his side, doubling up into a fetal position, clasping his wounds with his functional hand.

Parker started to sob. "I'm gut shot. I'm gonna die. You bitch. You've killed me."

"Yeah. You're going to die. Just like Minnie. But I've heard gut shots take a spell. When you're gone, I'll roll you out where the buzzards can find you. Pirate's already done part of their work. You can meet up with your friends in hell soon."

Chapter 37

C LAY HAD LEFT his mount with Audra at the Cimarron campsite after they heard gunfire on the mesa. They had arrived not more than an hour earlier, hoping that Ted Colmes might be waiting there. "Too much coincidence," Audra had said. "Outlaws, our detectives. Colmes on the loose someplace. I don't think somebody's hunting turkeys up there on the mesa."

"Not likely," Clay had agreed. "I'll take a gander. I'm sure there's a horse trail to the top someplace, but I'd like to get the kinks out of my bones anyway. Take me a little more time to hike up there, but I'll be less a target in case somebody takes a notion to toss lead my way. Why don't you hole up here someplace and wait for Colmes to show up? If I find trouble and need help, I'll fire three shots. Noon's not far away. Go ahead and eat. I likely won't be back till late afternoon. Maybe I'll have good news."

"And maybe you won't," she had replied.

He wasn't far from the top of the mesa when he sat down on a rough boulder to rest. It was a panoramic view from here, a beautiful mosaic of various shades of reds and greens and browns, miniature towers and ribbons of blue. Far more pleasant from this spot than from the back of a horse wandering through the harsh and sometimes barren land. He took a healthy drink from his canteen, rationalizing he would not need as much water going downhill on his return. He got up and soon walked out onto the mesa.

There had been no gunfire since he started his ascent. Was it just some cowboy passing through and coming across a deer? Unlikely. This did not seem like a "pass through" kind of place for a traveler. It would be a climb to nowhere as far as he could see. He quickly came across a trail where others had passed. He could not match Ted Colmes as a tracker, but during his time with the Tenth Cavalry, he had learned to read sign passably. Nobody was trying to hide their passage here. Impressions in the grass, which he guessed as moccasins. One walker wore cowboy boots. There was a third set—an animal, wolf-size. Perhaps, the other hikers had been scaring off a wolf with the gunshots. But it seemed unlikely a single wolf would be stalking humans.

He had one answer a short time later, when a dog's threatening barks broke the silence ahead of him. He could not see the animal for the cedars and junipers that were unusually thick at this juncture on the mesa. He moved slowly now but did not raise his Winchester. He knew dogs better than most and would be careful with his moves. Soon he came upon the dog some twenty paces distant on the path, watching, daring. A big devil, maybe the biggest he'd seen. He stopped, deciding to bide his time, ease the animal's concern. There had to be an owner someplace, and he wondered if he had walked blindly into a trap. Some of the Blue Bandana bunch?

"Stay put, mister." A female voice. "Set your rifle down on the ground. Then, real slow like, the same with your pistol."

He obeyed. "I'm not here to cause trouble." He got a glimpse of the possessor of the voice, partially hidden by the trunk of a giant cedar off to the right between him and the dog. She had a Winchester aimed directly at his chest.

"I hope not. I've killed two men in two days. Don't force me to make it a third."

Who in the hell was this? Some Calamity Jane? Some folks thought Negroes were fair game anytime, so he decided to play the only card he had left. He tapped on the badge pinned on his vest, although he knew she could not see it. "I'm with the Pinkerton National Detective Agency. I've got my badge right here."

"So you say. What in the hell are you doing clear up here?"

"I'm looking for somebody."

"Who?"

"A young woman who was abducted by train robbers. Her name is Maddie Sanford."

There was a long silence. "I'm Maddie Sanford."

Clay relaxed. It had been a longshot, but she had seemed the right age, and there had been nothing to lose by tossing out her name. "Can I come forward, so you can see my badge?"

"I guess so. But walk real slow and leave your guns behind."

Clay walked down the path toward the dog, the animal watching every move with alert yellow eyes. It had to be part wolf. Normal dogs did not have eyes like that. The young woman emerged from behind the tree and walked toward him but did not lower the rifle. "Take off your badge and toss it to me. You got any other proof you're who you say?"

"I got papers in my inside vest pocket."

"Open up your vest wide, so I can see and take them out."

She wasn't very trusting, but he guessed she had cause. He pulled the small wallet out of his pocket and unpinned his badge and tossed them on the ground in front of her. She was only about ten feet away, and he could have rushed her and disarmed her when she bent over to pick up his credentials. Of course, the dog would have him for supper if he tried it.

She looked at his badge and credentials for a bit and then lowered the rifle. She extended her hand with the items, and Clay stepped forward and retrieved them. He stuffed the wallet in his vest pocket and pinned on his badge while she watched.

"You can get your guns. Just remember, Pirate's keeping his eyes on you. Cabin's up the trail. We can talk there. You hungry?"

"I missed lunch."

"We can share a can of beans and peaches. And don't pay any attention to the dead man. Maybe you'd help me move him later."

He followed her to the cabin with the strange-looking wolf dog trailing him, obviously still suspicious of the new visitor. When he saw the young dead man in the yard, he thought anyone seeing the young man's mangled corpse would think twice before intruding on this young lady and her hound. This was a presumably spoiled railroad heiress?

They shared the beans and peaches sitting Indian style on the ground in the warm sunshine. While they ate, Maddie related a nutshell version of her ordeal following the abduction. She choked up some when she spoke of her friend, Minnie. She turned cold when she talked about Moon Parker, whose bloody corpse lay in the dirt not more than twenty feet away. He sensed there were omissions in Maddie's story, but he did not press. The girl was safe. That's all that mattered.

"I can bury Parker," he said, "if there's a shovel here."

"There's a shovel, but he's not to be buried," she said firmly.

Clay chose not to respond.

"I'd like you to help me drag him away from here, out in the open over that way, near the edge of the mesa, where the buzzards or any critters can eat him in peace."

"I see." He thought about her plans. What did it matter? After all she had been through, she was entitled to make such choices. "Okay, let's get it done."

After they had dragged the body to a rock shelf overlooking the Cimarron River and returned to the cabin, Clay said, "Maddie, the Pinkerton Agency has been hired to recover the gold, also. I have another operative with me, Audra Scott. You and Audra will get along just fine. We have another man with us who knows this country and who's looking for Copperhead Canyon. We expect him to meet my partner and me and lead us to the canyon where we expect to have two other agents waiting."

"I won't return to the canyon, but if you find the stream I told you about and follow it, you will find the canyon."

"About your not returning to the canyon, I've been thinking about that. Would you be willing to wait here until we come back? Right now, we don't have an extra horse, and the Copperhead Canyon venture could be very dangerous."

"And what if you don't come back?" Maddie asked

"Wait at least six nights. Do you have enough to eat?"

"Yes. What do I do after six nights?"

"It's a long trip but follow the river northeast. You will come to the old Santa Fe trail. If you encounter a family, see if they can help. Stay away from riders, alone or in a group. Keep the river in sight. It will take some days on foot, but you will eventually pass farmsteads, where you might find good folks who will help you get in touch with the law and your family. At worst, someday, deeper into Kansas, you will reach Ulysses. There is a U. S. Marshal posted there. Find that office, and you'll be safe."

"I'm not afraid to stay here with Pirate to look after me. And for some reason, I like this place. It's like I belong here. I'll do what you say. I expect you to come back." She shrugged. "But if you don't, I'll find my way home. Of course, I don't rightly know where that is right now."

Before he departed, Clay and Maddie repaired the door, using some of the former occupant's tools. The door would not withstand a prolonged battering, but it was sound and would keep the critters out and hold up long enough against human assault for Maddie to get her rifle ready and for the big dog to spring into action. He felt she was safer at the stone cabin than with the detectives at Copperhead Canyon.

Maddie was standing in the doorway, the wolf dog sitting at her feet, when Clay was ready to depart. He smiled at her and shook his head. "You've got grit, young lady. As the old timers say, 'you'll do to ride the river with.'" He turned and strode away.

Chapter 38

A S THE AFTERNOON wore on, Audra grew increasingly concerned about Clay. She reminded herself that she had heard no more gunfire. She took that as a positive sign. And where was Ted Colmes? Trace and Darby were out there someplace, and they couldn't take on the Blue Bandana outfit without backup. She paced the campsite she had chosen but had not set up the pup tents or done anything beyond gathering some firewood. She had put off lighting a fire until Clay returned.

Finally, she spotted Clay working his way down the rocky slopes below the mesa. He negotiated the rough trail gracefully, she noted, which was no surprise. He always moved with ease, almost catlike in coordination.

She strolled toward Clay as he neared the mesa's base. "I was worried about you," she said. "There weren't any more gunshots, but there are other ways to kill some-body."

He was smiling when he joined her. "Well, I guarantee it's dangerous up there for the wrong people, but I passed the test. I'm one of the good guys."

"You're making no sense whatever."

"I think I'm due a bonus. I just found Maddie Sanford. Had lunch with her as a matter of fact."

"You're not serious?"

"Dead serious. She was doing the shooting we heard."

"Then where is she?"

"She's staying up there till we come for her. And she's got a wolf dog big enough for you to saddle and ride if we need an extra mount."

Clay was feeding her just enough tidbits to make her crazy curious. "No more games. Just tell me the story be-ginning to end."

They sat down in the shade of one of the cottonwoods that lined the riverbank near the beginning of the incline to the mesa's top, and Clay told her about the adventures of Maddie Sanford. When he was finished, he added, "Maddie's a tough gal, let me tell you. I didn't have second thoughts about leaving her up there on her own, espe-cially given the few options we've got."

"Are you certain she's who she says she is? That she's Maddie Sanford?"

"Who else could she be? No, I don't have the least doubt I met up with Maddie Sanford. I'm guessing Maddie is a darn strong lady at her roots and grew up real fast during her ordeal. It doesn't matter. She will never be the same. Things happen to us, and we shoot off in some direction we would never have guessed. We learn what we're made of. Those with an iron core survive and adapt. The glass dolls break."

"Yes, I can attest to that. Changing the subject, have you noticed the dust off to the south across the river?"

"Yep. Looks like a single rider coming our way," Clay said.

"Ted Colmes?"

"I hope so, but I think maybe we should move back into the trees some. We're good targets sitting here like a pair of ducks."

They slipped away from the riverbank and into the trees and waited, watching the plume of dust move their way. When horse and rider neared the river, Clay said, "It's Colmes. We can step out so he sees us."

When Colmes approached the south side of the river, they waved. He saluted acknowledgment and urged his mount into the shallow water. After the horse clambered up onto the north bank, he dismounted and led the gelding to where Clay and Audra waited.

Colmes said, "I gambled you'd be here by now and headed for the mesa as soon as I found the canyon. That was last night. I didn't turn up Trace and Darby anyplace, but that ain't surprising. In case they had guards posted at the canyon rim, I wasn't inclined to look too hard. Besides, I'm guessing Trace and Darby wouldn't have been there yet—maybe tonight, or tomorrow."

Audra asked, "How far is the canyon from here?"

"Eight or nine-hour ride the way I come. Rested my horse and me last night and didn't push him much riding here. Didn't know how soon you'd want to be heading out."

"As soon as we can," Audra said, "but I know your horse needs at least several hours rest. What's the country like? Can we do this in the dark?"

"The land could be hell's home place, as far as I'm concerned, but we can thread our way twixt the rough spots now that I've scouted it out."

They agreed to go ahead with the fire and make a pot of coffee to help get them through the night ride. They still had three of Grandma's cinnamon buns left, and Audra came up with some apples she'd picked up in Ulysses. As they ate, Darby told Colmes about the discovery of

Maddie Sanford on the mesa top, omitting details she determined irrelevant to their mission. She was surprised when Colmes said he had met the man who built the stone cabin.

"I found the place back in '68 when I was scouting for Custer before the massacre," he said. "Guy that built it was an old mountain man. God, he seemed like he was older than the mesa then. White hair and beard. Shriveled up old guy. Missing a thumb on one hand. I spent a few hours with him, wormed out a little information. Indians never gave him trouble, he said. He brought stuff in on mules to trade for furs. Made a trip out spring and fall. He said the Indians thought he was wrong in the head and protected by the spirits, and he never discouraged the notion."

"Do you remember his name?" Clay asked. "I'm sure Maddie would like to know."

Colmes thought. "Yeah. George. George Wolf. Wouldn't have remembered, but he had a big wolf at the house. Better trained than any dog I ever seen. Hell, probably a great-great grandpa of that wolf dog you talked about. Man fancied wolves for sure. Said he had a wolf bitch in the cabin getting ready to whelp, so we couldn't go in. I suppose his way with wolves is something that kept the Indians back, too. He seemed happy there. Mentioned having squaws and kids in his trapping days but all dead from poxes the whites brought. Seemed at peace, though. Content with his life. Crazy? Like a fox maybe. Sounds like he knew he was dying and turned all his animals out and propped the door open so the big dog could come and go as he pleased. Probably knew the dog would stay till he died and beyond. Animal like that wouldn't starve."

Chapter 39

DARBY AND TRACE were nested in a cluster of rocks overlooking Copperhead Canyon, Trace surveying the canyon with his telescope. Trace calculated he had a half hour at best to gather his intelligence. The sunlight was fading, and shadows from the canyon walls were already beginning to creep over the floor.

"It's like a little village down there," Trace remarked, "but occupied by a dozen shacks scattered haphazardly, most north of the stream that runs through the canyon . . . the one we followed here. Lot of activity. Looks like about ten to twelve men going back and forth. Almost appears like serious packing's going on." He handed the spyglass to Darby. "Take a look, Darb. What do you think?"

Darby pressed the telescope to her eye and cast it back and forth for some minutes before commenting. "They're packing, but they're not pulling out tonight. The horses and mules are all in the remuda not far from the canyon entrance. There's a natural corral where the walls jut back and form a smaller dead-end canyon. They've got brush piled along the open side with double rows of ropes strung across the access and anchored to posts to hold the animals in. Not much grazing for that many, but I suppose they stake them out near the stream during the day. I see two buckboards near the north canyon wall."

Trace said, "The Pinkerton report said the gold shipment was hauled off in a wagon that was abandoned at the river later. Stands to reason they'd have others. They would have to haul food and supplies in from time to time. Do you see the wagon ruts entering the canyon?"

"Yeah. They must angle to the north. We didn't see any tracks coming in from the east and south."

"Colmes said the Cimarron cut-off for the Santa Fe trail swings south along the west part of No Man's Land. That might be where the wagons go to connect with their destination."

Darby continued roaming with the spyglass. "There's a cabin on a little rise with what looks like a storage building attached. Men seem to be traipsing back and forth to the building and picking up supplies there."

"I noticed," Trace said. "Two men left the cabin earlier. Another stood in the doorway watching them head down the hill. Sort of reminds me of a military command center. There's a wagon road that goes up to the front of it and then loops back. The building is probably where the supplies get stored and distributed."

"I wonder if the gold's there?" Darby asked.

"Hard to say. It's been several weeks since they hit the train and took the girl. The gold could have been moved out by now. The girl . . ."

"Do you think she's dead?"

"I hope not. But she would be able to identify the men and would have some idea of the location of the place if she wasn't blindfolded while they traveled. And if the Blue Bandanas were going to try to offer her for ransom, it's likely we would have heard something before we left Denver. It will be a miracle if we find her alive."

Darby put down the telescope. "I'm convinced they're getting ready to pull out of the canyon, probably in the morning."

"We don't care as long as they leave a live Maddie Sanford and the gold behind."

"Dreamer."

Trace said, "If we had the rest of our crew, I think we could pin them down here. The canyon's a good hideout, but it's a trap if you get caught in it. We should try to keep them here."

"And you've got something in mind?"

"It's getting dark now. We'll wait an hour or so and slip down and open that rope gate that corrals the horses. Just release the post hitches so it looks like somebody didn't tie the ropes tight. We won't make a racket, just let the mules and horses wander out on their own. One of them will find the open gate and lead the parade out. That will shake everybody out in the morning, and we can count heads while they're rounding up the animals . . . and buy time for our guns to show up."

"Eventually, they round up the horses," Darby said, "and get ready to move out. What then?"

"We start shooting and hope they take cover and stick around. You and I aren't going to be able to take prisoners without some help. Hopefully, Audra and the guys will show up on the other side of the canyon. I think they will figure out what we're trying to do."

"And if they don't show?"

"We'll think of something else. My old Sharps works just fine from this range."

"Well," Darby said, "I can't do much more than make noise with the Winchester from here."

"Noise will help. We want them to think they're surrounded by the Army."

"I doubt if two guns would do that."

They waited till after dark when a cloud covered sky hid the moon and stars and turned the canyon into a black hole. Then they departed their rock perch, and after checking their staked mounts, Trace and Darby wound their way down a deer path that led to the canyon opening. Trace had planned to make the trip to the corral alone, but Darby insisted on joining him in case they encountered a guard, or one of the Blue Bandanas spotted him and he needed cover fire.

It turned out to be a simple task, however. Trace crept up to the crude gate, unhitched the ropes from the post, let the ends drop and walked away. A curious gelding had approached to watch him untie the ropes and, as soon as the ropes fell away, stepped over the fallen barrier and started the exodus.

Trace and Darby, after stopping at a cluster of cedars, where they had stashed saddles and gear, picked up bedrolls and the last of the jerky, and returned to their hideout in the rocks. They felt secure at the location but wanted to leave nothing to chance and agreed to sleep in two hour shifts till dawn.

Chapter 40

"TRACE, YOU HAD better take a look at this." Trace opened his eyes, surprised to see a flow of glittering gold cascading over his wife's shoulders as the first rays of morning light cast its glow on the canyon rim. Darby was propped up on one knee, her back to him, with the spyglass pressed to her eye. Damn, it was his watch. She was scheduled to have awakened him at least an hour ago.

"You were supposed to wake me for my watch earlier," he grumbled.

"I wouldn't have slept anyway, and you were sleeping so soundly. You looked like an innocent little boy."

"I'm far from a little boy."

"Most of the time. But you're certainly far from innocent. Get over here and look at this."

He untangled the blankets and crawled to her side. She handed him the telescope, and he raised it to his eye.

Darby said, "Somebody must have seen that the horses were out."

"Yeah. Likely somebody got up to take a leak and saw movement or heard a whinny where it wasn't supposed to be."

"Some are still out rounding up their mounts, but a team of mules is already hitched to one of the wagons, and some old man is driving it up the lane toward the cabin with the storage building."

"Yeah," Trace said, "I see that. And everybody's spooked, looking over their shoulders. Not quite sure somebody didn't turn the horses loose. They're scurrying about like firemen headed for a fire. Looks like my judgment about letting the horses out wasn't so good."

"Don't fault yourself on your judgment."

"My dad always said, 'good judgment comes from experience, and a lot of that comes from bad judgment.'"

"Your father had a bit of wisdom for every occasion, it seems."

Trace chuckled. "Yeah, I guess he did. I ought to put it in a book. John Crockett was a wise man."

"Well, son of John Crockett, wise man, what do we do now?"

"Keep an eye on the wagon. I want to know what's going in it. Did you get a count on the men down there?"

"They're never all clustered together at the same time, so it's hard to tell, but I'm sure there aren't any more than a dozen. But there are at least three women flurrying about, but they're older. Two are on the stout side, and one has an emaciated look. Maddie Sanford is not one of them."

"Six apiece. We can't bring in that many ourselves. We'll have to take the numbers down."

"Do we need to move further down the canyon wall? I know you said the Sharps has the range, but you've got to see your target to hit it."

"I can see the men moving around, and I can get a bead, but some targets are more important than others. I'll need you to be sort of a spotter and tell me the location of the one I should take down."

"I don't know how I'd know which one."

"For instance, I don't want to take down the boss man. He's our link to the head of the snake. I think we'll be able to tell when things start happening."

"I'll try."

Trace said, "The men are gathering outside the house right now. Something's happening." He focused the spyglass on the doorway. "Man at the entrance. Black Stetson, black vest. Taller fella. Carries himself straight, like a soldier." He handed Darby the spyglass. "Get a fix on him. I don't want to take him down if I can keep from it. Spare the old man, too, if he's not causing trouble. We might need a muleskinner."

"There's another man with a black beard," Darby said. "He seems to be giving instructions to some of the men. I'd pick him as a keeper."

"Okay, your turn to make the judgments."

"I'm not sure I like playing God. Hey, four men are going in the cabin with the guy you picked as the boss."

"Let me see."

She gave him the telescope. The doorway was empty by the time he got it focused. He waited. Soon the man in the black vest and Stetson walked out, and the four men followed carrying a thick wooden platform, maybe about four feet square, he guessed, comparing it to the size of the carriers. But it was the cargo on top of the platform or rack that interested him. It was covered with what appeared to be a canvas wrap, but he had no doubt about what lay underneath.

He turned to Darby. "They're loading the gold on the wagon, Darb."

"All of it? Well, we can't count it from here, but it looks like they're headed back for more."

After the men stacked the fourth platform on the wagon, they did not return to the cabin, but they fell into a line outside. The presumed boss went into the house and returned with three full large bags in his arms, which he set down at his feet. He opened one of the bags and started pulling out smaller sacks filled with what Trace guessed to be gold coins and started passing them out to the men as they filed by.

"Payday," Trace said. "The gold bullion is loaded, and it should be all, or at least most, of it. They're going to be clearing out of the canyon. The wagon will have guards, but we can't chance them getting away from here. We've got to take out as many of this outfit as we can." He returned the spyglass to Darby. "Time to go to work."

He retrieved the Sharps, knelt behind a boulder and readied the gun to fire. "Pick a target," Trace said.

"The man with a rifle standing at the corner of the wagon. I think he's a guard. Another man nearer the cabin off by himself."

Trace sighted, squeezed the trigger, and the Sharps exploded. He fired again.

Darby said, "Both men down. One's not moving. The one near the wagon is rolling around on the ground. Everybody's running for cover. It won't be so easy now."

Rifle shots echoed through the canyon. Darby said, "They're shooting at us, but they haven't seen us. They're just guessing. And I think they're using smaller rifles, like Winchesters. Not much threat where we're at."

"No, but there are too many. We can't just ride in there and say, 'You're under arrest.'"

"Trace, there are two men headed for the horse corral. I wonder if they're going to try to work in behind us."

More gunfire from the canyon. Two men fell.

"I think the cavalry has arrived," Trace said. "Target the spyglass on the far side."

Darby swept the telescope across the canyon's north rim and found nothing. She lowered the instrument, focusing midway up the canyon wall, and finally found Audra, rifle butt pressed to her shoulder, perched on an outcropping of rock protruding from the northwest wall that she had somehow reached. Below her fellow operative, the wall tapered off, and loose rocks and shale could be ridden to the canyon floor, but the steep cliff above was best suited for a mountain goat's descent.

Nearly a hundred feet east, but settled higher on the wall, she focused on Ted Colmes, posted on a ledge that connected with a narrow trail to the top. She could not locate Clay, but she assumed he was secreted someplace.

She reported her findings to Trace, who removed his hat and wiped the sweat from his forehead.

Trace said, "We've got the bastards pinned down. But now what? We're hardly in a position to carry on a two-week siege."

"They've lost four men," Darby said. "The odds have evened some, and we're best positioned. Do you think they might be willing to talk surrender?"

"That's the best idea I've heard." Trace got to his feet. "I'm going to have a chat with those folks."

"And I'm going with you in case they don't want to talk."

They collected their mounts, and a half hour later rode into the mouth of the canyon. They reined in and wheeled their horses at the sound of a gunshot behind them. A bay gelding raced toward them, dragging a rider whose foot was caught in the stirrup. The horse galloped past, the rider's body bouncing over rocks and tree stumps. If the man wasn't dead when he fell from the horse, he was by now, Trace thought. He tensed when he saw another rider breaking through the trees that partially shielded Copperhead Canyon's entrance. He slipped his Colt from its holster, then re-holstered the gun when he saw Clay Sibley in the saddle.

Clay nudged his mount toward Trace and Darby, nodded and tipped his hat. "Howdy Mister and Missus Crockett. I was hoping we might have a get-together at this place."

Trace said, "Clay, your visit's very timely. I take it that the man riding off his saddle was going to give us a little welcome."

"He had you in his sights, but I'd been watching him for a spell. I guess he was posted as a sentry out here. He was going to die soon anyway. When you folks came along, I had to speed things up. Where you headed?"

"I'm going to call on the cabin where the boss man seems to hang his hat. See if they might just like to put down their guns and save their lives since we've got a twenty-man posse spread out above the canyon floor."

"Do you expect him to believe that?" Clay asked.

"He might, and he might not, but he won't be sure of it. It's a worth a try."

"And what if his answer is a bullet in the gut?"

"That's your job. I thought maybe the two of you might ride up that way with me, and when we get within rifle range, Darb can fan out to the left and you to the right. Audra and Colmes will be watching from up the wall. Whatever's left of the Blue Bandanas are hunkered down. I don't think anybody will make a move more than once or twice."

"Worth a try, I guess. It would be nice to get this place cleaned out fast."

"We haven't seen anything of the girl. Keep your eye out for her."

"Already found her. She seems fine. Glad we came across her. She'd have probably walked home on her own—her and a huge wolf dog she picked up—and we would have missed out on the bonus."

"That sounds impossible," Darby said.

"Well, you're not going to believe this gal and her story. If she had another three or four years tacked on her age, I'd recommend you hire her fast."

"Where is she?" Trace asked.

"She's waiting for us at that black mesa Colmes spoke about. Don't worry, she'll be fine there."

"Well, you've checked one project off the mission list. Another is sitting on buckboard behind a mule team just waiting to be picked up, so let's get down to business, if you don't mind."

Chapter 41

TRACE REINED HIS buckskin forward and they soon picked up the wagon ruts that led to the headquarters cabin. "Time for you two to split off," he said. "Stay as far back as you can and still keep me in sight and be within range of anybody who wants to fight."

Darby and Clay broke off and reined their mounts away from the trail. Trace shoved his Sharps in its saddle scabbard but unfastened the strap that anchored the Colt in the holster, patting the pistol grip for reassurance. He did not intend to be a stationary target if everything turned sour. He rode Atlas at a walk on the hump between the wagon ruts. He passed a ramshackle cabin to his left some twenty-five or thirty paces back from the trail, he estimated. A man peered out from one side of the win-

{307}

dow, careful not to expose his body. His weapon wasn't in sight, so he did not seem to be an immediate threat.

A rifle cracked twice from off to Trace's left. Darby. He looked back over his shoulder and saw the window observer's body draped over the sill, his rifle lying in the dirt beneath his dangling arms. Darby had made Trace's opinion inaccurate.

Another man near the wagon jumped up and aimed his rifle, but three shots from the north canyon wall drove into his back, and he dropped his rifle and staggered toward the headquarters cabin a few steps before collapsing facedown. Trace caught sight of another man under the wagon, but a glimpse of a white beard told him it was the muleskinner, who showed no signs of looking for a fight.

When Trace reached the wagon, he dismounted and hitched the buckskin stallion to a metal bracket on the sideboard. He casually lifted one of the canvas tarps to confirm the contents, looking it over like a man choosing from a pile of melons. He nodded his head with approval and turned toward the cabin. "Hello, the cabin," he yelled.

The door opened a crack. "Who are you? What do you want?"

"My name is Trace Crockett. I'm an operative for the Pinkerton National Detective Agency. I have other agents and a posse from Garden City surrounding the canyon. You've lost most of your men. I'll have my people move in and dispose of you and the rest if it's necessary, but I'm giving you an opportunity to surrender. You and anybody else in there, toss your weapons out and come out with your hands raised, and we'll talk. Now what's your name?"

"Bart Wince." According to Jim-Bob, this man was the immediate director of the gang's operations, the only link to those at the top. He was a prize, but he would need incentive to cooperate. Trace decided he would have to think about that. First task was to be sure they had the remaining gang members rounded up.

Bart Wince dropped two pistols and a rifle outside the cabin door, and then he opened it and stepped out with hands raised above his head. He walked slowly toward Trace. He was a man of medium height and build, and a carefully trimmed, heavy moustache, graced the flesh above his thin upper lip, dark-colored like the hair and sideburns showing under his gray Stetson's brim. As he drew closer, Trace saw no fear in Wince's pale blue eyes. This was a man he would have to persuade by reason.

"Anybody in the house?" Trace asked.

"No."

"Why should I believe you?"

"I've got nothing to gain by lying. You obviously have guns trained on us. If somebody comes out shooting, he's dead. But I might be, too."

"Call your men out, and then we'll talk."

Wince yelled, "All right men, come on out. Leave your guns behind. Pass the word. Gather at the wagon."

Then Trace hollered, "Pinkerton agents, I need you here now. Posse members, stay in place with rifles ready." He hoped Audra heard and that Colmes understood he was to remain on high ground overlooking the canyon floor in case somebody did not surrender and was foolish enough to position for a shot or try to escape.

Trace said, "You can lower your hands. Time to talk."

Wince leaned back against the wagon sideboard. "I'm not much of a talker."

Darby and Clay approached the wagon now, and Trace turned to them. "I hope Audra heard me and comes down. We need to inventory prisoners and cinch them up some way to travel. There are some women, too. They're not prisoners, and I guess they can stay if they want, but I don't know how they'll survive through a winter here on their own. And there's some burying that the prisoners can do. I'm wanting to talk with this man. Do you mind taking care of the others, with the idea we want to head out of here by mid-afternoon? We'll travel at night some if we need to."

Darby said, "You deal with this gentleman. Leave the rest to us."

Trace turned back to Bart Wince. "You said you're not much of a talker. Then listen to me for a spell. Here's how I see your situation. The gold bullion is now in custody of the Pinkerton Agency. Your Blue Bandana Gang is near extinction. The survivors, including you, are going to be turned over to the law along with any personal funds. I noticed you paid out money to your men this morning. It won't have time to get warm in their pockets."

Wince shrugged. "That's no surprise."

"Do you realize how many killings the Blue Bandanas have been responsible for?"

"I didn't ride with the men. I didn't kill anybody."

"If you're the boss, you'll hang with your men. It won't be long before everybody's talking so fast, we can't keep up with them. It's always like that when they come to realize the only way they can save their own skins is to start talking, and the truth be damned. There's not a man here that will own up to killing somebody. I don't peg you as a half-wit, Wince. We want the top man in the operation. You help us snag him—or her—and we'll make the law aware of your cooperation, and I'll testify that it's

Ron Schwab

my opinion you didn't kill anybody. I can't promise what happens after that, but I thinks it's unlikely you'll hang. Where there's life, there's hope, they always say."

"I don't know that much."

"Tell me what you do know. Help us, and we'll help you. Tell me about Newton Cromwell, for instance."

That caught Wince's attention. "Newt? How'd you know about Newt?"

"The Pinkertons aren't infallible, Wince, but we keep an eye out for betrayal. I suspect Cromwell is now in custody of the United States Marshal's office in Denver, along with anybody else in the agency who might have been helping him."

"Cromwell was my contact."

"There must be somebody else. Cromwell's a weasel, but I don't see him as the big boss of an operation like this."

"If you've got Cromwell, I guess I've got nothing to lose by telling you what I know. You said you'd speak up for me. That still goes?"

"It still goes."

"My contact with Cromwell was always in Trinidad. A few days from here by horseback. Add a day by wagon if you hit the Santa Fe cut-off north of here. There's a trail that branches off the cut-off that takes you pretty much straight west to Trinidad. I met Cromwell there sometimes. Others, I just picked up his telegram at the telegraph office. We had kind of a word code that hid the message from somebody that didn't know it. For instance, 'party' meant 'robbery'—that sort of thing."

"When did you last see Cromwell?"

"That's been a few weeks. Right after the big job, where we got the girl. It caused problems we weren't expecting. I came back here to check on how the job went. When I found out, I headed right back to Trinidad. Cromwell was already waiting there for me."

"What did he have to say?"

"Said we probably had to kill the girl. Too much risk for ransom. She could identify most of the gang. Knew where the hideout was. He said to guard her tight, but there was another job and to stay till he sent a telegram on that. He headed back to Denver by the AT & SF, and that was the last I saw of him. Got the message with details of the gold shipment and headed back to Copperhead Canyon to get word to one of my crews. I was here a day and returned to Trinidad to wait for instructions. That's when I got the message to take care of unfinished business—I assumed that meant the girl—and then close down the canyon, settle with the gang and deliver the gold shipment. It wasn't in our usual code, just fuzzy enough nobody would know what we were talking about."

The direct order to kill would have had to come from Wince. Trace knew the girl was safe someplace, but he asked anyway, "So, did you have the girl killed?"

He shook his head vigorously. "No. No. She escaped with some whore a few of the boys had here. Three men went after her. They should have been back by now. I don't know what the hell happened to them . . . or the girl and the woman."

"And what about the gold you had stashed here?"

"I'm to take it to Trinidad and set up camp at our usual meeting place. He said somebody would find me."

"Will you lead us to this place and have your mule skinner drive the team and wagon?"

"I guess. Gramps won't be a problem. He's never been anything but a muleskinner for the outfit. Bax Corker, one of the crew bosses could be trusted, if you want somebody else from the gang. He'll be looking for a deal and isn't a killer, if you know what I mean. Most of the others left ran with the other crew leader, Arlo Shales. I think he's got some serious paper out on him and likely has got nothing to lose by making a break for it or trying to turn the tables on you."

"Okay, you talk to this Gramps and Corker and clue them in that they can help themselves by helping us."

Chapter 42

WHEN HE CHECKED to see how the roundup of the remnants of the Blue Bandana Gang was progressing, Trace was glad to see Audra had come down from the canyon wall. He was not pleased, however, to see that Colmes had abandoned his station and appeared to be engaged in a fuss with Darby. He walked toward them, noting that Clay and Audra were on the ground tying lengths of rope together, leaving knotted loops about every fifteen feet in the string. He could not figure out what the purpose was, but his questions could wait.

He came up to Darby and Colmes and heard Darby say, "That's stupid. It will slow us down and stink worse than an overflowed privy hole."

"What's the trouble?" Trace asked.

Darby said, "He wants to take the bodies with us. I say they should be buried here."

Colmes said, "I want pictures. My main pay's the bounty money on any of those men. I'm entitled to take them in, or you're breaking the agreement."

"Will you see to their burial?"

"I will. You can deduct the costs from the Pinkerton salary I'll have coming."

"It appears we'll be heading to Trinidad. That's a good three days. Hot ones. There's one other wagon and mule team, I guess."

"I've set aside that for the three women," Darby said firmly.

Trace wasn't about to challenge her. She was going to be unhappy with his thoughts, anyway.

"Okay. Colmes, you'll have to strap the bodies to horses. Collect some blankets from the cabins to wrap them in. They're your responsibility. And you'll have to stay at the rear of our procession with your trophies and keep your distance."

He looked at Darby, who was glaring at him and biting her lower lip, as she was prone to do when she struggled with choking back words. "Will that work for a compromise, Darb? We did make a deal."

"Thanks for backing me up," she said, spinning and walking away to join Audra and Clay.

Damn, he hated that. They hardly ever fussed, and he didn't have any experience peacemaking with her when something like this happened. He turned back to Colmes. "We're pulling out in two hours. You'd better be collecting and loading your cargo, Colmes."

Chapter 43

THE CARAVAN STRUGGLED the first segment of the journey from Copperhead Canyon. The ground offered no consistency, first rough and rocky, then smooth-going prairie, fading into dust before giving way to rock again. The worst of it was the Cimarron River, which was congenial to the mounts in the shallows where they crossed but less kind to the buckboards. The women from the outlaw hideaway had to be removed from the wagon mid-river and carried by horseback to the riverbank before the mule team, driven by Bax Corker, was able to pull a wheel loose from a mud pocket. The gold wagon almost tipped over when the load shifted, and Trace and Clay, with a few of the prisoners, had to wade into the water and fight the current to move some of the bricks before getting the wagon's balance restored.

Once across, they soon hit the Santa Fe cut-off, and the bizarre parade of riders moved on without resistance. The gang overseer, Bart Wince, was accorded some preference and allowed to ride without bonds. The other prisoners not pressed to wagon duty rode single file joined by a rope with a loop pulled snugly about each rider's neck. Behind the prisoners rolled the two wagons, and fifty feet back Ted Colmes rode with his macabre string of horses packed with corpses.

Darby and Audra guarded the captives with Colmes available in the unlikely event some escape attempt occurred. Trace was out front some distance and out of sight, looking for a suitable night camp, and Clay had departed with a spare saddled mare to recover Maddie from the mesa. Colmes had informed him of a trail on the mesa's north side that Indian ponies and likely the late cabin occupant had used for access to the top.

Darby was feeling a bit guilty for snapping at Trace the previous afternoon. She knew he was a natural commander, and his military background made him the logical leader in their present circumstances, but she was also accustomed to decision-making and had chafed at being reined in. He had apologized contritely last night, and that was another thing she loved about him. He would not permit differences to turn into a long, cold war. And, of course, she had swallowed hard and admitted his decision was right.

They had ended up staying the night in Copperhead Canyon. The gathering of food supplies and preparation for the journey to Trinidad had taken unexpected time, and, as it turned out, they never would have crossed the Cimarron or found habitable campgrounds before nightfall. As it was, it had taken most of this day to cross the river and reach the cut-off. Dark would be descending in another few hours.

Audra reined in beside her. "This day has been a challenge. Trace and Colmes think we'll have three nights on the trail before we reach Trinidad. That counts tonight. We can't get there soon enough, as far as I'm concerned. We've got to prepare meals for this riffraff and escort them to take a poop or piss. And then there's that stench drifting up from the back of the caravan. We should have buried those bodies."

"That's what I thought, but Trace convinced me that we'd made a deal with Colmes. We don't need to feel obligated to give him a bonus for the job."

"I hope Clay can make it back with Maddie Sanford before dark."

"You seem to worry a lot about Clay lately."

"Well, I like him."

"He likes you, too. A lot, I'd say."

"What makes you say that?"

"I'm not blind. I see how he watches you."

"Well, we have become good friends. He said he's got my back, and he's proved that more than once. When this is over, are you going to offer him a chance to stay on with the agency?"

"I take it you would be a 'yes' vote?"

"Well, yeah. We're partners, but I still think of you and Trace as the agency bosses."

"Trace and I have talked. We agreed that if you didn't object, we would try to take Clay on."

"I don't object."

"I didn't think you would."

Later, Darby saw Trace coming toward them on the trail and trotted Cinnamon ahead to meet him. When they approached, she could see a satisfied smile on his face, so she took that as a sign he'd discovered a decent campsite.

When she rode up to him, she said, "Your face says you found a stopping place."

"Yep, about fifteen minutes up the trail."

"Good. Audra and I are tired and hungry."

"Well, you're aways from eating. Got to get everybody settled in and fires going. A lot of beans and biscuits to bake for this bunch."

"We're going to take advantage of the slave labor tonight and put the prisoners to work at fires and ovens. We're not chuck wagon cooks. They can do their share and maybe more," Darby said.

Chapter 44

AUDRA WAS SEATED by a fire when Clay and Maddie, trailed by the wolf dog she had heard about, entered the clearing among the Cottonwood grove where camp was set up. It was nearly midnight, and she had informed Trace and Darby she would wait up a spell. She had been about ready to give up and head to her bedroll when Clay appeared with the newcomers.

She got up and waved, and Clay and the girl dismounted, hitched their horses to a few saplings and walked over to the fire. Audra had to restrain herself from rushing to Clay and giving him a hug, so she turned her attention to the girl, who approached with her hand clutched to Clay's forearm. Audra stepped forward with her arms extended and embraced the girl. "I'm Audra Scott," she said, "and I know you're Maddie. We're so glad to have you with us. Welcome."

Maddie, after hesitating, returned the hug. "Thank you. I feel I know you. Clay spoke so much about you."

Audra could not help but wonder what Clay had said. "Come sit down. If you're hungry, I've still got beans and biscuits, and coffee, too."

The girl had felt like skin and bones, Audra thought. She guessed that Maddie might stand a half foot taller than herself but probably did not weigh an ounce more. She had obviously been through rough times. Clay went to put up the horses, and Maddie and Audra engaged in small talk while Audra heated the coffee and food. By the time Clay returned, she felt she and Maddie were comfortable with each other and would get along fine. She was not going to press the girl for details but made it known she would be a willing listener.

After she had handed Clay and Maddie tin plates and told them they could serve themselves and feel free to toss Pirate a few biscuits, she said, "I told Trace and Darby that if I was up when you came in, I would wake them. There are things we need to talk about."

Clay said, "We'll be fine. Thanks for putting out some grub. We didn't take time to eat this afternoon—didn't bring much with us to tell the truth."

When Audra returned with her partners, the young lady had to endure more introductions, but Audra noticed she was more at ease now, probably adjusting to the realization she was no longer on her own and among people who would protect her. She seemed barely able to hold her eyes open after eating, and Audra asked her if she would like to share her pup tent and go on to bed. Maddie nodded agreeably and picked up a ragged buffalo robe she had been sitting on.

"I have a few extra blankets, if you want to use them." Audra said.

"No, thank you. This stinky old robe and I been together through some hard times. Is there room for Pirate in the tent?"

"Of course," Audra said, not mentioning that there might not be room for Audra with the monster wolf dog lodging there. It didn't matter. Whatever made Maddie feel safe and comfortable. She escorted Maddie and Pirate to the tent, where both collapsed. She could have sworn they were both asleep before she turned away and returned to the fire where the others waited.

Trace and Darby were seated on the ground now, each with a cup of coffee, Darby leaning her head against Trace's shoulder. Audra claimed her former isolated spot, wondering what it would be like to be snuggled up to Clay.

Trace said, "We need to talk while we're all together. I don't know what opportunities we'll have the next few days. I'm thinking we're going to need to split up for a spell when we get to Trinidad, and I don't like it. If we go marching into town with a string of prisoners and another string of bodies, word will be all over town in an instant about the Blue Bandana Gang's demise. Odds are that word gets to the top man if he's there to collect his gold bullion."

"And he's gone before we ever meet up with him," Darby said.

"I had in mind, Clay, that you and Audra would stay an extra night outside Trinidad a few miles. Colmes, too. Gramps and Bart Wince will take the wagon to the meeting place and wait. Darb and I will follow some distance back. Wince said the place is in a hilly, wooded area, that we should be able to move in without being seen. I wanted to ride alongside the wagon as a guard, but Darb's worried I might be recognized."

Clay asked, "You think the head of the snake is somebody who knows you?"

"I don't know. Tell them your theory, Darb."

Darby said, "What's a man going to do with two-pound bars of gold bullion? That many dollars' worth? He can't cash it out without a bank or any other business knowing it's stolen. He must know how to get it smelted."

"Smelted?" Audra asked.

"Melted down and cast into some other form without the identifying numbers. Disks. Small blocks. Something that makes it unrecognizable so it can be moved in small quantities, if necessary. I'm wondering if this could be masterminded by somebody at the Mint office. They would work personally with a smelter and whoever cast the original bricks. For a share, such an operation might smelt and recast. Somebody in the Mint office could easily have become acquainted with folks at the Pinkerton office and Cromwell in particular."

Clay asked, "Do you really want to risk leaving Wince alone with that gold for whatever time the wait goes on?"

"I don't like it."

Audra jumped in. "Clay and I wouldn't be recognized. We were never at either the Pinkerton or Mint offices." She knew she was proposing a huge test of trust, but she was confident she and Clay could handle it.

"They'd be suspicious of a woman," Trace countered.

"I can tie up my hair, cover it with my hat."

Darby said, "I could give you a moustache." Darby, a onetime actress before diversion to school teaching and then to the Pinkerton agency, worked with disguises and carried a bag with supplies sufficient for minor appearance alterations. She turned to Trace. "I know you want to be there, Trace, but Clay and Audra can do this."

Trace still looked doubtful. "Okay, and Ted Colmes will go with you. I'll personally lead the corpse parade."

Chapter 45

C LAY AND A mustachioed Audra rode on opposite sides of the buckboard. Gramps handled the mule reins, and Bart Wince sat on the seat beside him. An ill-tempered Ted Colmes trailed the wagon. He had at first refused the assignment. He had been determined to deliver the bodies and arrange for photographs of the corpses and prisoners to support any reward claims. Darby had verbally ripped him to shreds, declaring that Pinkerton would file the claims for reward money if he failed to complete his commitment to the job. Breach of contract, she had insisted. Under Darby's attack, Colmes had melted into a whipped pup and relented. But Clay could tell the bounty hunter still seethed. He hoped he could still be counted upon if trouble came. Cornered, he guessed the man would have no choice.

Gramps seemed to know where they were headed. He had doubtless made the trip before. The wagon bounced over deep ruts, twisting into grass carpeted hills. The ruts suggested a trail once heavily traveled, but the long grass and absence of horse excrement hinted that the trail had few trekkers these days. Clay was surprised when the wagon made a sharp turn and rolled into a vast open area that included an old shack leaning toward collapse and the opening to an abandoned mine carved out of the stone cliff that rose abruptly and signaled the trail's dead end. Coal had once been mined here, he assumed from the black chunks scattered about the ground and several rusted, abandoned carts resting near the mine opening. He saw no sign of the three riders that belonged with the horses tied to the hitching rail near the shack.

Clay did not like this spot. They were boxed in by steep hills on three sides. Their only exit was the entrance. He looked over at Audra, who returned his gaze with a worried look. He saw her hands moving to ease her double-barreled shotgun from its scabbard. He gave a quick nod of approval and unfastened his Colt's holster strap.

He tensed when he saw a stocky man emerge from the mine, a cocky, confident sort, Clay judged from his strut and the pistols slung on both hips. He appeared to be Mexican, although his skin was darker than Clay's own. He presented a false smile surrounded by scraggly moustache and chin whiskers. His hat was of the broad-brimmed, oval-crowned Plainsman style. He also cradled a Winchester in his arms.

The man walked up to the front of the wagon, his froglike eyes focused on Wince. Clay wished he could see Wince's face. "Buenos dios, Bart. You have easy trip?"

"Buenos dios, Pablo. Easy, yes."

The Mexican tossed the rifle to Wince and with a cross-draw reached for his pistols. It looked fancy, but that was all. The blast from Audra's shotgun tore into his chest before the pistols left the man's holsters. Wince swung around in his seat with the rifle aimed at Clay, but Clay's Colt planted a slug in the man's forehead before he could get off a shot, and he tumbled off the seat, landing between the mules' legs. Gramps had dropped in front of the seat, hands clasped to the reins when the shooting started.

"Don't shoot," the old man said, as he crawled back on the seat. "I ain't part of nothin'."

Another shot cracked behind them, and Clay turned to see a body rolling down a hillock. A grim-faced Colmes sat astride his mount with his rifle raised. "You're welcome," he yelled.

Colmes reined his horse up closer to the wagon. "Maybe there's more reward money with this bunch. We can haul some fresh ones to the undertaker."

"There are three horses," Clay said. "One man's not accounted for, and I don't think we killed the big boss, if he even showed up."

Gramps volunteered, "They stay inside the mine when they're here. Never seen the boss man. Don't know if he ever comes here. Newt somebody usually met us here when I was along. 'Course, most of the time I was fetching supplies in town, and Bart rode out on his own to talk to Newt or whoever he was meetin' up with."

"Audra, let's take a look at the mine," Clay said. "Ted, maybe you can keep an eye out here."

Clay and Audra dismounted, and Audra loaded another shell in her shotgun, so both barrels would be ready to fire. They spread out, each moving forward on opposite sides of the mine opening. They were walking toward a black hole, and for all Clay knew, somebody was waiting under cover of the darkness with a shotgun or other weapon, waiting to take them down if they were fools enough to give him an easy target. On Clay's hand signal, they each angled out to the far ends of the cliff face and then began inching along the cliff wall toward the mine entrance.

When they had both reached the entrance, Clay yelled, "Hey, you in there. Your men are all dead, put your hands in the air and walk out, and you'll live to see another day."

Silence. And then an explosion echoing through the mine.

"What in the hell?" Clay said.

"Do you think . . ?" Audra asked.

"I don't know. I'm not ready to get my head blown off trying to find out just yet."

"There's got to be a lamp someplace. They don't just wander around in the dark in there." She leaned her shotgun up against the cliff wall, dropped to her belly and started to worm her way into the cave.

"Audra," Clay protested. "Wait."

She ignored him, and when only her feet were outside the tunnel, her body started moving backward. When she emerged, she held a kerosene lantern in her hand. She got back to her feet and displayed it proudly. "Figured they'd have to have lanterns just inside to light up when they entered. Got a lucifer?"

"Yeah." He tossed her a little pouch he kept in a vest pocket.

Audra lit the lamp, "We can't wait all day. I don't think that shot came our way. Just keep me covered."

Trace had warned him that the woman had an impulsive streak and was too quick to take risks sometimes. As Audra stepped into the tunnel, holding the lantern in front of her, Clay fell in beside her. They immediately saw the man to the rear of the wide entry area, sprawled on the stone floor, a short-barreled pistol beside him. Clay moved ahead and knelt beside him. Bleeding from a bullet hole in the temple. Death had been instant. He studied the dead man. He was attired in new blue denims and a leather jacket, but he was not a man familiar with physical labor. Hands free of blisters or callouses, pale, clean-shaven face. He was a slender, narrow-shouldered man, who obviously earned his living inside four walls.

"He doesn't look like the head of a snake," Audra said.

"Maybe he's not. But, as they say, appearances can be deceiving."

Chapter 46

TRACE HAD BEEN surprised when Colmes returned early afternoon and reported that Clay and Audra were on their way to Trinidad with the gold wagon and four more bodies. Colmes had informed him that the Pinkerton detectives were uncertain of the identity of the dead men, Wince excepted. One man was suspected of being the general or big boss.

Within thirty minutes of Colmes's arrival, the caravan pulled out for Trinidad, relegating Colmes and the rotting corpses to the rear again. In less than an hour, a wide-eyed crowd, many observers pinching noses, gathered along the main avenue to watch a parade that would grow with each retelling.

Darby pointed and said, "Trace, the gold wagon's up there. I see Clay and Audra near it." Trace reined the buckskin around and trotted the mount back to Colmes.

When he reached him, he said, "There's an undertaking establishment off to your right. Make your arrangements and get this stinking mess off the streets. Then come get the others. If you're short of funds, talk to Darb. I'm sure she'll advance it." Then he turned away, feeling like he was already soaked with the stench of death.

Trace dismounted and led the buckskin up the street toward Darby, who had led the procession to Clay and Audra. They stood in front of a building with a sign above the door that said "Marshal" and were speaking with a rather dapper-looking gentleman wearing a suit and derby hat.

Trace walked up, and Darby turned to him and said, "Trace, this is Bat Masterson. He's the City Marshal here in Trinidad."

Trace stepped forward and shook Masterson's hand. "I've heard of you. Dodge City lawman. Buffalo hunter, scout. I had no idea you were marshal here."

"Just took on the job. Told the council it would be temporary." He tendered an impish smile that was not quite hidden by the thick, neatly trimmed moustache. "I was told Trinidad was a quiet town when I took the job. You folks showing up has turned that into a tall tale."

Trace was surprised at Masterson's apparent youth. He couldn't be much past thirty, yet he was a legend in his time. Masterson and a brother had supposedly cleaned up Dodge five or six years back. But Trace had been told by a friend who operated a Dodge livery stable that the former lawman had been chased out of town by threat of a lynching for killing a man there not too many months ago.

"Well," Trace said, "I guess my partners have clued you in on what we're dealing with."

"Yep. My deputies are filling up my jail with the few Blue Bandanas you left alive. The undertaker's helped himself to all but one of the dead men. Miss Scott said you and your wife need to take a gander at him. He's stretched out on the floor just inside my office. You can look him over, and then I'll have the undertaker pick him up and take his picture. After that, I expect you'll want to see the Trinidad Bank about locking up that gold."

Trace and Darby walked into the marshal's office with Masterson. The body lay on the floor, wrapped in a blanket. Masterson bent over and pulled the blanket away from the dead man's face.

"I'll be damned," Trace said.

"Horace Youngblood," Darby said.

"And who is Horace Youngblood?" Masterson asked.

Trace said, "Director of the government's mint office in Denver. High level bureaucrat. Head of the snake, it appears. He would have all the right connections, especially with a renegade Pinkerton agent at the Denver office and a gold smelting firm." He turned to Darby. "With Youngblood dead, I'm guessing Cromwell's tongue is going to loosen up and fill in any blanks."

"That's not our worry," Darby reminded. "We've about finished our job. Time for the law to take over. And I think the home office will have some house cleaning to do in Denver."

"We'd better talk to somebody at the bank," Trace said. "Marshal Masterson, we appreciate all you're doing for us here. We'll see to notification of the U. S. Marshal's office in Denver, and I'm sure they'll relieve you of your prisoners soon."

"Just call me Bat. I'd be grateful if you would give me a report before you leave town. For overnight, you might find the Trinidad Imperial a nice change for your party. They have hot baths and fine dining available."

When Trace and Darby stepped outside, Trace said, "Masterson mentioned baths. Do you think he was trying to tell me something?"

"If not, he should have."

He ignored her remark. "What are we going to do with the three ladies in the wagon? They didn't seem to be a part of the robberies. They were just hired on to pleasure some of the men as near as I can tell. But we can't just dump them in the street."

Darby said, "I've been thinking about that. Each of those men was carrying a pouch full of double eagles, well over a thousand dollars' worth, enough to live on for a year or more if you're careful. It would give somebody a healthy fresh start. What if we'd lose three of those pouches?"

"It will likely end up with the government. Nobody knows which job that money came from. I think those ladies would make better use of it."

"I'll take care of it. Do you and Clay want to take care of getting the gold into the bank vault? I'll see if Audra and Maddie can make arrangements at a livery for this herd of horses and mules. I need to send a lot of telegrams and wait at the telegraph office for answers. I think I'll just let Audra see if she can sell the spare livestock and tack, and, of course, the two wagons. I want to go home, and I'll see about train connections for us and our own horses."

"What about Maddie and that wolf dog?"

Darby said, "I'm taking them to Manhattan with us. I'm not sending her to the witch in Denver. We'll notify her father, and he can come there to pick her up. I'm not sending her off on the train by herself. Not after what she's been through. I suppose we'll have to do some finagling to get Pirate in her hotel room tonight. I don't know if she's willing to give up the buffalo robe yet or not."

"Are you still okay with hiring Clay for the Crockett Agency?"

"Absolutely, if I can handle the negotiations."

"I never thought otherwise. Speaking of negotiations . . ."

"Yes?"

"It's been a spell. What are my chances if I take a bath tonight?"

She looked up at him, fluttered her eyelashes and winked. "Pretty good, I'd say."